Praise for Nicole Aus

"With a mix of romance, SandM and menage, this story has something for everyone who enjoys erotica...This story starts out hot and never lets up."

~ *Romantic Times Book Reviews*

Rating: 5 Hearts   "Nicole Austin has a real talent for creating dynamic couples with intense connections and the best intimate scenes imaginable!   This reviewer would read and recommend anything Ms. Austin writes!"

~ *Mandie, Loves Romances and More*

Look for these titles by
Nicole Austin

Now Available:

Tamara's Spirit

With TK Winters
Mimosa Night
Margarita Day
(Combined in print under the title of Intoxicating Desires)

Jesse's Challenge

Corralled Book Three

Nicole Austin

A SAMHAIN PUBLISHING, LTD. publication.

Samhain Publishing, Ltd.
577 Mulberry Street, Suite 1520
Macon, GA 31201
www.samhainpublishing.com

Jesse's Challenge
Copyright © 2008 by Nicole Austin
Print ISBN: 978-1-59998-960-0
Digital ISBN: 1-59998-684-1

Editing by Angela James
Cover by Anne Cain

First Samhain Publishing, Ltd. electronic publication: November 2007
First Samhain Publishing, Ltd. print publication: September 2008

Dedication

This one's for you, Candy. Thanks for keeping me on track, Sugar-Girl. Your honest opinion, suggestions and research assistance are worth millions. Your friendship is a priceless gift which I'll always treasure!

Prologue

Jesse Powers stared out the sliding glass doors but saw nothing.

Leaving his friends and normal way of life behind in Montana to pursue a dream had seemed such an easy decision. A real no brainer. He would stand on his own two feet and make it in a completely foreign environment without a hitch.

Yeah, right. Lord, he had so much to learn.

What did he think he was doing smack dab in the middle of the Denver business jungle? He was a fish out of water, floundering in an attempt to survive without a snowball's chance in hell of actually doing so.

Jesse was a good ole country boy who belonged in worn denim and dusty boots, not custom tailored suits, fancy spit-shined leather shoes, tight-collared shirts, and ties that came close to choking him. He had no business trying to order something edible from the indecipherable menus in elegant frou-frou restaurants while rubbing elbows with serious movers and shakers.

Even though they treated him with the utmost respect while vying for the pleasure of having him pay for their overpriced services, he detected an undercurrent of disdain. They weren't buying the act. He wasn't fooling anyone, least of all himself.

What he wouldn't give to be back at the ranch. He pictured himself sitting in the bunkhouse with his feet propped up on the old wooden table and a longneck beer in his hand, shooting-the-shit with the guys. Instead he stood here, staring out into space as a crew of movers set up expensive rented furniture he didn't even like in a highfalutin' apartment he despised.

If things went well here, he'd be able to return to the ranch and manage his business without ever having to leave the comfort of home. All he had to do was navigate these uncharted waters, avoid the sharks, and then hightail it back to the Shooting Star and his friends.

Simple, right? He'd thought so.

Problem was he'd not imagined how alone and out of place he would feel. In the middle of endless, sleepless nights, Jesse would find himself returning to the website he'd helped Steph design for the ranch's horse breeding program. He'd stare with overwhelming longing at the pictures of his home, listening to Savannah's familiar voice on the recorded message over and over. It wasn't anywhere close to being there, but did provide a small measure of relief.

As he was about to turn away, a flash of color and movement in the building across the way caught his eye. Maybe this apartment wasn't so bad after all. It afforded him an unobstructed view into the bedroom of a goddess. Fuck yeah!

The sultry redhead was unbuttoning a white blouse as she walked into the room looking all hot and bothered. Without closing the blinds over the sliding glass doors, she walked closer. Standing facing him, she dropped the blouse into a silky puddle at her feet, then slender fingers dropped the zipper of a bronze mini-skirt and it too joined the discarded top.

Fuck. He'd never seen anyone half as gorgeous as the beautiful temptress. Jesse felt kind of sleazy for watching, but he wasn't about tear his gaze away from the fiery woman. There was something about her, other than being almost naked, which captivated him.

She stood wearing the sheerest pink bra and panties, which hid nothing from his hot gaze. He clearly saw the dark circle of her areolas topping the most amazing set of tits. Aw, gawd. He could even detect a deep red patch of hair between long legs that went on forever. A garter belt spanned her narrow waist, holding silk stockings in place.

Jesse imagined removing her panties with his teeth, then bending her over the footboard of the bed. The spiked heels she wore would put her at the perfect height to be taken from behind. Her silk stockings would brush against his legs while his hard cock slammed into the tight grip of her pussy.

Or better yet, he would take her against the wall, those luscious legs wrapped around his body, pulling him deep into the saddle created between her thighs just for him. He'd ride her hard for hours until they were covered with sweat and exhausted.

Hell yeah! What a phenomenal ride she would be.

Even from the distance between them, he noticed her nipples were puckered in invitation, pressing against the thin covering. She stood with her head hanging back, arms held out and the flow of air from the ceiling vent ruffling the long, thick mass of dark red hair over her creamy skin. Damn, how his fingers ached to drift over her bared body.

So beautiful and confident. She appeared to be secure and comfortable with her body, abandoning herself to the hedonistic delight of the cold air rushing over bare flesh.

His cock hardened and felt ready to burst right through the thick denim jeans. With deft fingers he opened the button, relieving some of the constriction, and stroked over the thick ridge while observing the ethereal angel across the way.

She was a classy woman. Someone who belonged on the arm of a powerful, successful businessman. Absolutely way too fine for a simple cowboy. He'd never have a woman comparable to her, but wouldn't pass up this chance to witness an unguarded moment with such a ravishing beauty.

Jesse wondered what she was like. Did she realize how gorgeous she was and walk with her nose high in the air, ignoring the common people around her? Did she spend her nights being wined and dined by the *crème de la crème* of society? Or maybe she was a little more down to earth. He sure hoped so.

As if she sensed his intense scrutiny, the seductive vixen slowly raised her head and looked right at him. Jesse was trapped, drowning in the most breathtaking pair of emerald green eyes. His mystery woman seemed unconcerned to be standing before him in her current state of undress. For the length of several heartbeats her gaze wandered his body with clear interest, then she smiled and he was lost. Plump, rosy lips spread wide to reveal a dazzling flash of white teeth and her whole face lit up.

Making no attempt to cover herself, the seductress made a slow turn on her heel and strolled away with the casual air of someone taking a walk in a quiet park.

He had no idea how long he stared into her bedroom, stroking his dick, wondering how to get a high-class broad such as her in his life. All Jesse knew was that he desired the flirtatious siren. Somehow, someway, he'd figure out how to capture the woman who'd just stolen his heart.

Chapter One

"Is he there? Watching?" Tink asked in a breathy tone.

"He's always watching." Kate chuckled, her voice sounded husky and aroused even to her own ears. "I haven't been alone since Tom moved in."

Kate could see straight into his bedroom as clearly as he could see into hers. She vividly remembered the first time she'd seen her hunky neighbor several weeks before.

Mister Tall, Dark, and Gorgeous had moved into the trendy Denver apartment complex on a swelteringly hot July day. By the time she'd completed the arduous commute through rush hour traffic, Kate had been beyond frustrated. She'd had a hellacious day at work dealing with her D.H.—dickhead boss. Having the movers whistle and ogle her as she climbed the stairs had been the final insult of an infuriating day.

It had started out pleasantly enough. Kate had woken hot and wet from a wonderfully vivid erotic dream of a sexy man with intense amber eyes. Normally, her faithful battery operated boyfriend was all she needed to take the edge off. But even B.O.B., accompanied by some of his closest friends, hadn't been able to help her that morning.

Because of her extended efforts she'd been running late. Trying to hurry, she'd dropped her brand new, very expensive tube of mulberry velvet lipstick onto the Italian tile bathroom floor. Of course, it had smashed into a useless glob.

A freshly manicured fingernail broke during the clean up. Then, as she'd rolled a pair of seamed French silk stockings over her legs, the jagged remnants of her nail had slashed through the sheer hosiery, creating an enormous run.

The day had just gotten worse from there. Nothing she'd done had pleased D.H. At lunch, a klutzy moron in the company cafeteria trying to get a better look down her top had spilled coffee on her dry-clean-only skirt. Then she'd ended up missing a deadline because her teammate had dropped the ball. The final straw came during the bumper-to-bumper drive home when the AC in her convertible Mazda had gone on the fritz.

The wonderfully chilled air in the apartment had welcomed Kate home into its artic embrace. She remembered unbuttoning her white silk blouse as she headed into the bedroom. Uncharacteristically, she'd let it fall to the floor in a rumpled heap. Next she'd pulled down the side zipper on her mini skirt and allowed it to join the discarded top.

She had stood under the air vent wearing only a nearly see-through bra, matching thong panties, garter belt, stockings, and four inch high heels. Just imagining how wanton she must have looked sent a small shudder down her spine.

The cold air had instantly tightened her nipples, which poked out through the sheer bra. With arms spread out from her sides, her head had rolled back between her shoulders, hair caressing her lower back. Kate had surrendered herself to the incomparable ecstasy of central air conditioning.

The realization she was being watched had slowly invaded her senses, raising goose bumps over her skin. She'd lifted her head and looked directly into the most breath-taking pair of whiskey-colored eyes.

At first she drank in the perfect light brown halo of hair

surrounding angular features. The Stetson sitting atop his head at a rakish angle made him appear to be an untamed cowboy. His strong, square jaw framed a luscious pair of lips bracketed by deep, charming dimples.

The thick column of his throat led to broad, naked shoulders. Swallowing hard, Kate had allowed her gaze to caress golden skin covering well-formed pectorals, flat six-pack abs, and lean hips cupped in stone washed denim. The button and first few inches of his fly had been tantalizingly left open. Her gaze followed a light trail of dark hair that arrowed down into the narrow opening. She licked her lips at the memory of how the denim had hugged muscular legs.

Her new neighbor was sin-on-a-stick.

Tink's riotous laughter snapped Kate back to the present and their conversation. "Come on, Kate. Let me live vicariously through you. Give Tom a little show, and describe every delicious reaction."

Tink had begun calling him Tom, as in peeping Tom, when the man had continued his blatant watching. Although Kate wouldn't admit it to anyone, she had started intentionally leaving the blinds on the sliding glass doors open. Some wicked part of her wanted his attention.

"Tink! I can't."

"Listen to me, Kate. We're both gonna have some fun. Put me on speaker phone, then close your eyes..."

"Tink, there's no way I can do this."

"Just do it," Tink ordered sternly. "Damn it, Kate. Do it for me."

Taking a deep breath, Kate finally gave in to what had become her friend's almost daily request. This was not her idea. She did not want to turn him on, taunt him. Right?

15

No, she didn't. Tink's incessant pleading was to blame for whatever happened, or didn't. It was all Tink's evil inspiration and doing. Kate was a responsible, totally in control, modern woman. Focused and career oriented. Tink was the wild, wanton one.

Maybe Kate would even manage to convince herself this faulty logic was true. *Nah!*

"Fine!" She sighed deeply. "But if he turns out to be some serial killer psycho just remember this was all your fault."

"Sure, Kate. Whatever helps you sleep at night." Tink's voice had gone breathless with anticipation.

Kate dropped the phone into its cradle, and closed her eyes. Her back was to the glass doors. She'd revealed no sign of having noticed Tom there, watching, waiting.

Soft, sultry music came through the open phone line along with Tink's seductive instructions. "Let your body slowly begin to move to the music. Sway your hips gently. Let the rhythm take you away."

Following Tink's advice, Kate let her hands glide over lush, feminine curves. Each movement accentuated different assets. She knew her body looked good, and she took pride in her feminine allure.

"Just listen to my voice, and the music. It's just you and me, sugar."

Slowly Kate let herself slip away, trusting in her friend. Giving in to the erotic game.

"Are you still wearing the same outfit from work?"

"Yes." The rough and racy sound of her own voice startled her.

"Good. Now, move forward until you're standing in front of the cedar chest with your back to Tom. With your left leg straight, bend the right one, and put your foot on the chest. Let your back arch as your hands roam down your hips. Brush your fingers over your bent leg until they reach your ankle. When you're there, arch your neck and let your hair cascade down your back."

The words and music faded into the background as Kate put on a provocative show. In her mind it was Tom's big hands sweeping along the firm curve of her calf, teasing the soft skin of her slender thigh, and under the edge of the short skirt. It was his fingers pulling the camisole over her head, and unfastening the front clasp of her bra.

Kate let the lacy material slink down her back and drop to the floor. Tucking her thumbs into the waist of her skirt, she slowly dragged it over her long legs, teasing her skin and awakening nerve endings. She'd worn her panties over the garter straps, which made them simple to remove.

The intensity of his gaze scorched her flesh. Kate had no doubt Tom watched every move. She could feel the weight of his stare. Brief amazement that she didn't feel the least bit shy flittered through her mind before the thought melted away with a rush of juices coating her swollen pussy lips.

Wearing only the lace garter, stockings, and high heels, Kate followed Tink's directives. With her eyes closed, she turned to face Tom. Her manicured nails teased turgid nipples for several moments before taking the full globes into her hands to massage her heavy breasts. She held them out for Tom's appreciation, stroked them for his pleasure.

Kate froze for only a few seconds when Tink instructed her to sit on the edge of the chest and spread her legs wide, showing off the auburn thatch of downy hair in between, and her damp folds. Still cupping her breasts, Kate let her hair fall forward over a shoulder. She was careful to make sure the thick tresses did not block his view. With calculated slowness her tongue slid between her lips to flick the tip of an engorged nipple.

"Shit, this is so hot. I'd love to see the look on his face and what he's doing."

Again, Kate pushed her friend's voice to the background as she seduced Tom. The warmth of her tongue on her nipple created a fresh flow of arousal. Several languid circles around her nipple sent electrical impulses surging to her core.

"Mmm!" Kate moaned as she sucked the plump peak deep into her mouth then nipped lightly with her teeth. One hand flowed along her quivering belly to gently tease her mound. Using her thumb and pinky, she spread the plump lips wide. Her middle finger played from the bottom of her slit to her pulsing clit. She gasped as a nail skated over the engorged nub peeking out from its hood. Delicious throbbing sensations spread through her sex as the nail circled, tugging skin and nerves, spreading her secretions.

She slipped two fingers between the slick folds of her sex, sinking them deep into her pussy. The fingers produced a wet slurping sound as they skated through the thick fluid. Muscles fluttered and grasped as the achingly sweet sensations spread. Kate imagined they were Tom's thick, calloused fingers teasing her most sensitive flesh.

"Open your eyes. Tell me what he's doing." The last was more demand than request.

Kate complied and gasped at the sight of Tom in all his naked glory. "Oh my God!" She took a moment to drink in the sight, barely recognizing her own voice as she described the scene to Tink.

"He is buck-assed naked and staring right into my eyes. One fist is wrapped around his cock. Monster thing has to be at least eight...no, make that nine inches long." A sensual shiver raced down her spine. "His thumb just rode over the head, spreading his come over the shaft. Damn, Tink. It's so hard and thick."

She was panting now, but continued to describe every steamy detail. Well-sculpted muscles rippled sinuously beneath tanned flesh as he worked that enormous cock. He had the naturally powerful body of a laborer, not the molded bulk of a weight lifter.

Darkened bedroom eyes followed every movement she made. Kate felt the concentration of his gaze as strongly as any physical caress. She imagined the thrill of his work roughened hands all over her body.

"Holy shit, Tink. I've never seen such an enormous cock. I want to taste it so bad." Her breathing was erratic. "Swallow down every yummy inch."

Mmm, how she'd love to lave her tongue over the luscious length, teasing the thick veins. When she took him into her mouth the girth would stretch her lips. Fighting to take his entire cock would be a test of her skill, and damn if she didn't love a challenge. Almost as much as she'd love to suck on his beautiful dick.

Adding a third finger to those stretching her pussy, Kate followed his steady rhythm. Without a doubt, he was close. The large sac between his legs was tucked up tight against his pelvis, and his cock had grown bigger, almost angry looking.

Fucking her fingers, Kate pressed the heel of her hand against her clit. Bracing herself with the other hand behind her ass on the chest, her hips began to buck and grind, riding her hand.

Tom's strokes and hers remained synchronized. His tongue curled out to wet his upper lip, and he swallowed hard, Adam's

19

apple bobbing. His lips parted, and he clearly mouthed, "Come for me."

That was all it took. The blistering tension assaulting her body peaked, throwing her into scorching bliss. Hot come gushed over her hand. At the same time strong jets of milky semen shot from the tip of Tom's cock, splattering in a wide arc over the glass door.

Kate collapsed back on her elbows, letting her head fall back against the footboard of her bed. Blood pounded in her ears, and her chest heaved, struggling to suck in much needed oxygen. The tension of her stress-filled day lifted from her body on the wings of the powerful orgasm.

Over the speaker, Tink cried out her own release. To have shared this with her best friend was a bit odd, but Kate brushed off the slight discomfort. Their friendship had always been intimate and open. No need to get embarrassed now. Not when the experience brought them both gratification.

When Kate looked up again, her voyeur was gone. She silently thanked Tom for the collective release.

Chapter Two

By far, the best thing about the rented space was the clear view straight into his neighbor's bedroom. The spicy siren stole his breath.

Leaving the blinds open over the sliding doors had become habit. Jesse often woke in the middle of the night and stared into her room, wishing there were enough light to make out her shape beneath the covers as she slept. He'd also developed an obsessive practice of rushing to catch any fleeting glimpse of the woman he'd nicknamed Red whenever he walked through the door.

He loved to watch her strip off the business clothes at the end of a long day and slip into a slinky negligee. His conscience nagged at him for intruding on her privacy, but Jesse couldn't force himself not to look or fantasize.

Over the weeks she'd played cat and mouse with him. While he made no attempt to hide the fact that he watched, Red acted as though she had not noticed his rapt attention. He knew better now. She'd been leaving the blinds open more and more often. Each afternoon she put on a show of undressing down to her undergarments and touching herself just enough to drive him insane with lust.

Regardless of how busy he was with business, Jesse still found ample time to keep a close eye on his beautiful neighbor.

He liked to be there when she got home from work, watching as she shrugged the weight of the world off those slender shoulders. It stirred something deep in his chest.

But today was different. Today she'd managed to shock him. After his experiences on the ranch with Tamara, a woman he'd shared with the other cowboys, he hadn't thought anything could surprise him. He'd considered himself to be rather jaded from their wild escapades, but Red had proved him wrong.

Once again she pretended not to notice his presence, but something about her movements was different. Small hands slid over silky clothing as she moved in a seductive rhythm and the sly fox performed a naughty strip tease for him. This time she took off the bra and panties too, blessing him with the beautiful sight of her naked body.

He wasted no time shucking his clothes, and taking his painfully hard cock into his fist. Damn, he wished he was close enough to get a better look at her pussy. The need to taste the cream coating her fingers as she fucked herself for him was overwhelming.

Oh, Red. Today is the day, honey. He was through with games.

℘

"Oh, shit!" Tink gasped. "That was fucking intense."

The extreme understatement made Kate laugh. It was certainly the most powerful and blatantly sexual act she'd ever undertaken.

Delightful aftershocks burst throughout her still fevered sex, similar to miniature explosions. It had been a great appetizer, but only served to emphasize the empty ache in her pussy. She needed so much more.

Having a man around on a regular basis was such a hassle—took her focus away from work—but getting laid once in a while would be nice. It had been about ten months since she'd last had sex. Way too long to go without, in her opinion.

The memory of walking in on her ex-fiancé fucking his secretary on top of his desk still haunted Kate. Jerking off his engagement ring, she'd hurled it at Robert's head. After slamming the door on the horrible scene, she hadn't looked back.

The first messages on her answering machine from the snake had been pleading and apologetic. Then he'd tried to explain away what she'd walked in on as "meaningless sex". The messages had escalated to angry threats until she'd given the tape to the police and filed harassment charges. It had been the last she'd had to deal with him.

Since then Kate had dove into work and changed her priorities. Marriage and family were no longer foremost on her mind. Now she focused on advancing her career to the exclusion of almost everything else. Soon, all the effort would pay off. She'd get promoted at her job, get management experience and be ready to open her own company.

"That's gonna make a great letter to *Penthouse*."

"Don't you dare," Kate warned. Writing to the magazine was one of her bawdy friend's favorite activities. The two letters she'd managed to get published in the periodical sat proudly displayed on the center of the crazy woman's coffee table. Tink was so honored, she showed them to everyone.

Her wild friend sure kept things interesting.

When Kate finally sat up, Tom no longer watched through the glass doors. She was surprised by the sharp pang of disappointment which struck her. All that remained of him was the white streak of semen on the glass.

"Damn, he's gone."

"How about the same time tomorrow? That'll give me time to come up with a really hot encore."

Kate's laughter was cut off by loud banging on her apartment door. Panic flittered through her overwhelmed system as her eyes snapped back to the window across the way. He still wasn't there and she had no intention of answering the door since it might very well be Tom.

The pounding continued unabated.

"Aren't you going to see who that is?"

"Hell, no!"

Kate's heart slammed rapidly against her rib cage. Every muscle in her body filled with tension. "What if it's him?" She'd teased the big stranger without mercy. No way was she opening the door to him now. There was no telling how he'd react.

As suddenly as it had started the pounding stopped. She let out a sigh, relieved he'd given up, yet a bit of unexpected disappointment tightened her chest.

"Open up." The deep voice rolled through the apartment. "I know you're in there." A hard knock punctuated the statement.

Full blown panic seized Kate in its icy clutches. She sprung up, grabbing a short robe from the foot of her bed. "Oh, shit!" Her voice trembled with apprehension. "What am I gonna do?"

Tink was silent until the pounding began again. "Go answer the door, but leave me on speaker. That way I can call for help if anything happens."

"Answer the door," she sputtered. "What if he's some psycho serial killer?" Or worse. She knew what would happen if she opened the door. They'd have sex. No ifs, ands or buts about it. The desire was too strong to fight.

"Kate, you've been teasing him for weeks. Don't you think it's about time the two of you actually met?"

She belted the robe tightly at her waist. Glancing at her rumpled appearance in the full-length mirror, she combed trembling fingers through her hair. Damn, she looked freshly fucked and wanton. Exactly as she felt.

"I don't know if I can do this." Better to keep the door between them than give in to the hunger.

The next round of pounding sent nerve jarring sensations pulsing through her tense body. "He's not going away." Both fear and excitement tinged her voice.

"I'm right here with you, Kate. Go answer the door."

She walked through her normally soothing apartment with fingers of painful anxiety squeezing her heart. "Ah...just a minute. I'm coming."

Kate could have sworn she heard him mumble, "Oh, you will be," but must have been mistaken.

"Wh-Who is it?"

"Your neighbor." His voice sounded gravely. Sexy as hell.

When she hesitated, he spoke again, confirming her worst fears.

"I'm not leaving until you open the door, Red."

Leaving the security chain in place, Kate turned the dead bolt, then glanced through the small opening allowed by the chain. Peeking through the gap she came face to face with one very agitated, rough-and-ready cowboy.

"I think it's 'bout time we finally met, don't you?" It was more of a statement than question.

He stood more than six feet tall, towering over her slight, five-eight frame. Kate had to crane her neck and look way, way up to see his face. The hard chiseled lines of his jaw, coupled with the feral power in his eyes were both frightening and arousing.

No matter how gorgeous he'd looked from a distance, Tom was devastatingly handsome up close. His eyes appeared darker, smoldering with passion. The dimples she'd admired were even hotter than she'd thought. And talk about big. Oh my!

"I—um…nice to meet you, Tom. Got, ah…gotta go now."

Good Lord. She sounded like an idiot. It was way past time to cut this short, put an end to her distress.

His huge boot surged forward, stopping her attempt to close the door. "Who's Tom? Listen, I just want to talk, honey. That's all. If you'll feel better, you can leave the door open. I'll stay out here."

He seemed impatient as he waited for her compliance. When he finally moved his foot back, Kate closed the door, gasping for breath. For a moment she considered slamming the bolt back in place, then locking herself in the bedroom, but his voice shredded her resolve.

"Come on, honey. I won't bite…unless you want me to."

The mere idea made her shiver. *Bite me, baby.*

At the gentle coaxing of his seductive voice and teasing words, Kate unlatched the chain then slowly opened the door. Why she was following his commands she had no idea. There was something authoritative about the cowboy which made her want to comply with his wishes.

"That's better, honey. Now I can properly introduce myself. My name is Jesse Powers."

Wow, he really is a cowboy.

Kate drank him in like a tall, cool glass of water, quenching her parched senses. Her gaze roamed from the top of his black

Stetson to the toe of dusty black cowboy boots, absorbing every masculine inch. In his rush, he'd only buttoned half of his shirt, granting her a tantalizing glimpse of muscular chest dusted with a smattering of dark hair.

Damn if that wasn't one well-built hunk of man eclipsing her doorway.

When her gaze returned to those sinful eyes, Kate realized he was giving her as blatantly thorough of a once over. Then she remembered how little she wore. Oh well, too late to worry about it now.

"Kate Brooks." Her slender hand was engulfed in his much larger one. His sun-darkened skin looked exotic next to her milky white complexion. She'd expected him to shake, but instead, he turned her hand, lifted it to his lips and placed a soft kiss against her palm. She felt the tender press of his lips all the way to her toes, which curled into the plush carpet.

He was a strong man, but he touched her with tenderness. The thick fingers caressing hers intrigued Kate, made her wonder how they'd feel rasping over her sensitive nipples or the soft folds of her sex. A hot blush crept over her cheeks when she realized the dangerous path her mind traveled, yet trying to rein in her wandering thoughts was useless. Not with the incredible eye candy standing so close.

She continued to stare, mesmerized by his hands. His fingers were long, the flesh work-roughened. A worn patch of lighter-colored skin divided his thumb from the first finger of his left hand. They looked to be competent hands. Hands capable of delivering great pleasure.

Kate's body softened, melted.

When she looked into his face again a devilish smile curved those inviting lips. She found herself leaning into the warmth radiating from him, imagining sliding her tongue into the crescent-shaped impressions bracketing his smile.

"Nice to finally meet you, Katie."

She didn't correct him for calling her Katie. She didn't allow anyone to use the hated nickname, but somehow it seemed right coming from Jesse.

Before she knew what happened, Jesse had closed the door and maneuvered her into the living room. After setting her down on the suede couch, he knelt next to her legs, bringing them eye to eye.

He still held her hand within his, stroking his thumb over the inside of her wrist. The maddening caress sent sizzling sensations through her body, snapping every nerve ending to attention.

A brief spike of fear surged through her mind. She'd permitted a very large, powerful stranger into her apartment after masturbating for him. She knew nothing about Tom. No, not Tom. She now knew his name was Jesse, but nothing else. He could be a deranged sociopath for all she knew.

God, the amazing orgasm must have fried her brain cells and sent her common sense on vacation.

"No need to be afraid of me, honey. It's too late for that." Jesse tucked a few errant strands of hair behind her ear. "You're so beautiful, Katie."

She couldn't talk past the painful lump in her throat. While she was embarrassed over what she'd done, she was also excited by his larger-than-life presence. He smelled of fresh air, evergreens and aroused male.

Yum!

His velvety voice seemed to reach deep into her body, stroking long forgotten sensual pathways. The fingers holding her hand were warm and tender, sending those wonderful electrical impulses through her arm, keeping her ultra aware of his proximity.

In some odd way, his dimples inspired trust, giving him the appearance of a mischievous young boy. Mmm, but his hard body was all man. She was almost overcome with the desire to lean forward the few inches separating them, trace the curves of his lips with her tongue and taste his mouth.

"Keep looking at me like that and you may end up with what those green eyes are asking for, honey."

Tink's frantic voice attempted to break through the spell holding Kate captive.

"Kate? Christ, woman. Pick up the phone or I'm calling the police. Damn it, what's going on?"

Jesse's mesmerizing gaze held her rapt attention for several moments longer before he leaned back on his heels, breaking the spell. "You better go pick up the phone, Katie."

Pick up the phone? What was he talking about? She was about to ask him when Tink began shouting again.

"Shit! Okay, I'm calling the cops."

Her friend's frightened and shaky voice finally got Kate moving. She raced into the bedroom on trembling legs and grabbed up the handset. "It's okay, Tink. I'm fine. I just got...distracted."

Boy, was that ever an understatement. Jesse Powers was devastating to her senses. His sultry gaze had the ability to hold her enthralled, while his touch sent her reeling.

"Jesus, you scared the crap out of me, Kate. What the hell's happening?"

"I'm sorry, Tink. My neighbor, Tom...er, I mean Jesse, came to visit."

What the heck was she supposed to do with him now that

29

she'd seduced the man and acted the shameless hussy? She couldn't hide here in the bedroom and leave him sitting in the living room forever. Eventually she'd have to go back out there.

"Oh, my God. Did you let him in, Kate? What are you doing?"

"Good question, Tink. Hell, you got me into this. Got any bright ideas on how I should get out of it?"

Did she want to get out of it? If she were honest the answer was not only no, but hell no. She wanted more. More of his fingers touching, his lips tasting...

"I expect full, explicit, down and dirty details of what happens."

"Thanks, you're a big help." Before she could say anything else, Kate felt his presence. Turning slowly, she faced the bedroom doorway. Jesse's massive physique filled the frame. His penetrating gaze cut through all her natural defenses.

"I've gotta go now, Tink. He's standing at my bedroom door." Every fiber of her being seemed to turned into iron, and was reaching out toward Jesse as if he were a magnet. Something about him exerted a forceful pull on her.

Moving with the easy grace of a panther stalking its prey, Jesse invaded her inner sanctum. Kate was too intrigued to be truly scared. There was something commanding about him inspiring trust, invoking confidence, and making her feel safe. His masculine heat enveloped her as he moved to within scant inches of her aching body. She wanted to melt into him, trace every masculine plane and angle, sample each gorgeous attraction.

"Say goodbye," he whispered against her ear.

Goose bumps spread over Kate's skin. Every hair on her arms and neck rose as she gave in to his seductive energy. Her fingers loosened their grip on the phone as he took it away.

"Say goodbye now, Katie." It was a command she was unable to resist.

"Um...goodbye. Talk to ya later." She whispered the words into the phone, but for some reason didn't remember the name of the person she'd been talking to. Not that it mattered. She'd sort it out later. Much later.

Chapter Three

"Tell me what you want?" Jesse's teeth nipped at her lobe. His hot tongue bathed the delicate shell before moving to the ultra sensitive skin behind her ear.

How was she supposed to think at a time like this? The man held her under some kind of strange spell, slowing her reactions, consuming her mind and body. He overwhelmed every one of her senses. Not that she minded. It was a pleasant feeling, certainly something that had not happened before.

Insistent hands tugged at the sash tied around her waist. Before she grasped what was happening, the soft silk of her robe salaciously floated down her back, pooling around her feet. Sultry heat spread through her body as she stared into his eyes, darkened with lust.

"So beautiful!"

His gaze swept over her, while his hands skimmed down her arms. The rough calluses tantalized every tender inch of skin they touched, leaving raging need in their wake.

Kate had rarely been this excited. She'd never felt so totally attuned to anyone. This man affected her in more ways than she could begin to contemplate. She found him intoxicating.

"Katie." He murmured her name as his lips descended to claim her mouth.

There was nothing tentative or teasing in his kiss. His lips boldly captured hers and demanded entry. He seized control, changing her from a confident, assured woman into a floundering mass of need. Her nipples pebbled into diamond-hard peaks topping swollen breasts. Heat washed through her naked body, sending all her blood to her labia.

She gasped, and his diabolical tongue plunged between her lips. The hot organ devoured, caressed and invaded everywhere. It moved over teeth, reached the furthest recesses, and teased her palate. He kissed her thoroughly and completely.

Jesse cupped her ass cheeks, pulling her firmly against his solid frame. The thick length of his erection branded its impression on her soft belly.

Kate felt hot juices gushing from her pussy, coating her inner thighs. Her entire body melted into his much larger one. Sudden panic stopped her heart as her mind focused on what was happening. She'd let a virtual stranger into her home. He had her undressed and surrendering to his every whim.

This is insane!

All thought disintegrated and she whimpered as his wicked fingers kneaded and separated her ass cheeks. The soft cotton of his shirt rasped against her nipples, annihilating any resistance. The solid width of his denim clad thigh pressed between her legs, seeking entrance she was powerless to deny. She needed this. Needed him. Had needed him for the past few weeks since she'd started teasing and taunting him.

He dared attempt what none other had—to possess and control Kate. And that was exactly what Jesse did—quickly and effectively took control of her.

Under normal circumstances she retained rigid discipline at all times, staying focused on her objectives. She didn't allow herself to be stripped bare, literally and figuratively. But somehow this truly incredible man had managed to take charge in no time flat. His dominance was heady, wicked, wonderful and frightening all at the same time. Kate gave in, becoming absorbed in the ecstasy of his concentrated attention, and followed his lead.

Jesse was in seventh heaven. The sly red fox's response to his every touch was filled with amazing heat. She was everything he'd ever wished for and more. So much more.

Her long and curvy body melded into his as if they'd been made specifically for each other. Holding Kate was similar to holding a lighted stick of pliable dynamite. He knew when she finally exploded neither of them would be the same again.

He wanted to watch her orgasm over and over again until she pleaded for mercy. He'd fuck her pretty mouth, hot pussy, tight ass and then get creative. Jesse would take her every way known to man then invent a few new positions guaranteed to rock her world.

First, he *had* to taste her. It was an overpowering craving which defied resistance.

The warm cavern of her mouth welcomed every broad sweep of his tongue with the fresh, invigorating taste of peppermint and woman. Hers was a flavor he'd never grow tired of. Kate's tongue greeted his invasion. She alternated between making bold strokes and sucking him into her mouth. They kissed until both were gasping for breath, but still dying for more.

Jesse nibbled along her jaw, traced the shell of her ear then tongued the soft lobe. His hands skimmed over the firm cheeks of her ass, which filled his hands to perfection. Damned if she didn't start riding his leg as he pressed it between her luscious thighs. He held her tight, wishing his clothes were out of the way, dying to feel her skin against his hard sinew.

Between the hard peaks of her breasts brushing over his chest, and the trembling of her soft belly against his cock, Jesse was ready to come in his jeans. He needed some relief, a way to tame this out of control blaze. His earlier release had not been nearly enough. Jerking himself off didn't cut the tension. It only left his cock aching to drill into her moist heat.

He snaked a hand over her hip and between their bodies, briefly teasing the springy tuft of hair before dipping his fingers down to her swollen folds. She was wet, eager and ready.

"Oh God. You're so hot and wet for me, honey. Open wider," Jesse demanded.

It took a moment for Kate to respond before spreading her trembling thighs further. He caressed her drenched labia, spreading the lubrication then pinching the tender lips. The painful sting spread wild thunderbolts of pleasure through her body.

"Wider," he commanded.

She had no choice but comply. There would be no denying him anything. Kate was washed away, lost in the wildfire he'd started and stoked to a hungry, consuming blaze. A needy whimper escaped her as greedy fingers parted her slick folds. His middle finger stroked her slit, sending her reeling. When he exerted firm pressure against her pulsing clit, Kate nearly collapsed. Her thighs shook, all strength gone. The only thing keeping her standing was his muscular arms.

Kate knew she was in trouble here. The gorgeous cowboy had discovered and pushed all her buttons, leaving her a pliable blob of Jell-O, which he molded with consummate skill.

He teased, tempted and delighted her most tender tissues, waking up nerve endings she'd not known existed. Tingles surged through her body, coalescing in her abdomen as he whispered dark and wicked things against her ear.

"I'm going to suck on those pretty pale nipples, bite at them and watch as they turn red. I'll devour your luscious tits until you come, calling out my name, but I won't stop there. I'm going to lick, suck and nibble all over your gorgeous body, spending extra time on this succulent clit."

Jesse emphasized the words by pinching the bundle of nerves between his fingers again. Kate gasped as the tension coiled tighter. Hell, she could orgasm from merely listening to his naughty pillow talk.

"I want to watch those rosy lips stretch over my cock as I fuck your mouth, see you swallow my come. Before my cock drills into your hungry holes, I'll fuck them with my fingers until you're begging, sobbing for what you want...what you need."

Oh yes. Please. Now! She wanted everything he described. Longed to suck his cock, to taste and be filled by him. Fulfill her wildest fantasies. And she knew without a doubt he would deliver her into the arms of ecstasy.

"You want that, honey? Want me to take you to the gates of paradise and show you what lies beyond?"

Yesyesyesyesyes!

Jesse kissed, licked, and nipped his way down her elegant neck. He tried to control his baser instincts, but wasn't able resist the temptation to mark her, claim her like some Neanderthal man. The dazzling vixen was his now, he wasn't about to let her go. Not before they were satiated, used up and exhausted.

At the tender junction where neck met shoulder, along a light path of cinnamon freckles, his teeth plunged sharply into the soft flesh. Before the pain could register, he soothed the bite with his tongue. She tasted so sweet. He sucked greedily, basking in Kate's glorious raspberry-and-cream-scented skin.

"Jesse." She moaned his name, the yearning in her voice making his cock jerk.

"Mmm...right here, honey."

To prove the statement he drove two fingers into her moist cavern. Kate cried out as her eager pussy grasped at the invading digits, coiled muscles drawing them deeper. Jesse struggled to maintain control over his unruly body. His envious cock throbbed, wanting to sink into the silken grasp holding his fingers so tight, to feel the gentle pull of her damp flesh.

"Need more, honey? No problem. I aim to please." He spoke the oath against the upper curve her breast. Pulling out of her quivering flesh, Jesse took her ripe nipple into his mouth at the same instant he plunged three fingers into her grasping cunt. With his teeth, he lightly scraped over the elongated peak. In reward of his efforts, a fresh flood of hot juices gushed over his hand.

She was going to be the death of him. Kate gave as good as she got. Her hips met each thrust of his fingers, back arched, driving her nipple further into his hungry mouth. Lusty mewling sounds rumbled up from her throat.

God, he loved the sounds she made.

"Yes...please!" Kate begged, although he was sure she didn't know what she was asking for, what she wanted, who she needed. She merely responded to the desires he stirred.

That was unacceptable. Not at all what he wanted.

Jesse's conscience would not allow him to sink his cock into her hot pussy unless she realized who delivered each burst of passion. She had to want *him*, not some faceless, nameless dick. He had to be sure. He would allow no mistakes or regrets to come between them.

Damn, the wait was going to destroy him. If he didn't get his cock out of the painful confinement of his jeans soon, he was afraid there would be permanent damage. He pulled his fingers from her body and attempted to back away a step, gather a little breathing room.

Kate followed him blindly, keeping her lithe body molded against his.

"Open your eyes, honey. I want you to know, to see."

She whimpered and thrust her pelvis against his rock-hard erection, eyes clamped shut, lost in the frenzy he'd driven her to.

"Katie! Open up those pretty eyes and look at me."

Although she finally complied, Kate's eyes were glassy, the pupils dilated. Her deep red mane framed her face in wild disarray. All traces of lipstick were gone, lips swollen and red from his dominating kisses. She looked feral and sexy, the most beautiful woman he'd ever seen.

"That's it, honey. Look at me."

"Please, Jesse!" The raspy quality of her voice made his knees weak. And she'd said his name, but it wasn't enough.

"You don't know me, Katie. I'm not some limp-dicked weasel you can bend to your wishes. Some refined city boy who won't push you to your limits, test your boundaries. I won't be easy on you. I'll fuck you hard and demand your complete submission, take you in ways you've never imagined, require things you may not be able to handle."

Her eyes widened, and she looked scared. For some reason, that look made him want to shelter and pamper her, keep her by his side.

"Be sure, Katie. Is this what you want? What you're willing to give?"

She remained quiet for several long moments, looking up at him from heavy-lidded eyes. A wide range of emotions played across her face. Jesse saw raw primal need, a touch of fear and apprehension, dawning realization, and finally acceptance. Then she shocked him with her bold words, nearly driving him to his knees.

"I want you to fuck me long and hard. Take me, use my body every way a man can use a woman. When you push me over the edge, then I want you to start all over again. I want you to possess me completely, Jesse. You're exactly what I want."

In stunned silence, he stared at Kate. Never had a woman given herself to him so freely. The trust inherent in the gesture tightened his chest. He'd never imagined finding such a responsive, giving lover. A woman capable of matching his lust, challenging and demanding he give even more.

"Don't just stand there with your mouth hanging open. I thought you were going to fuck me."

The calm statement was a kick to his gut. Jesse narrowed his eyes as joy burst within him. His red fox sure had spunk. "Oh, I am going to fuck you, honey. When I'm done there will be no doubt as to who owns that sassy mouth and bodacious body. No one else will ever do after I'm done with you."

Then the incredible seductress really blew his mind. She moved in closer, and covered his jean-clad cock with her slender fingers, stroking his length.

"You have too many clothes on, Jesse. I want to see what I'm getting out of this deal."

Any sanity Jesse still had snapped. Kate was proving to be a strong, courageous and fascinating woman. Not even his last lusty lover, Tamara, could hold a candle to the brazen siren who taunted him now. She was sublime, feminine perfection in a sinful body he had no power to resist.

With an animalistic cry, Jesse ripped his shirt open, sending buttons scattering across the room. Quick, savage movements removed the barrier of his jeans. He stood naked before her, allowing Kate to look her fill.

"Get on the bed," he ordered.

Kate stood her ground, a sly smile curving her lips. She wasn't going to let him overwhelm her and have complete control. Good! He loved her feisty spirit.

Gazing at the solid wall of man standing in her room, she couldn't prevent a sharp gasp from escaping. His cock was bigger than she'd imagined. Bigger than anything she'd ever seen. It jutted out proud and firm from a nest of dark curls, the crown so heavy it weighed the shaft down. His large sack appeared tense and full, drawn close to his body.

His cock jerked under the sustained scrutiny and Kate reveled in the heady response. She grinned and imagined spending long hours exploring all that glorious male flesh. Her blood fired as vivid images filled her mind. In the shower, water sluicing over his skin as she attempted to suck his long cock all the way down to the root. In her bed, sweat slicking muscle as she rode him to completion. Between her spread legs, firm ass cheeks flexing as he powered into her...

"Get on the bed now or I'll tie you to it." The warning broke her paralysis.

Kate turned and jumped onto the bed, bouncing a bit before lying on her back, thighs spread wide. There she waited. Jesse took his time, sauntering across the room. The primal look in his gaze seared her skin.

His intention was clear in the depths of those feral eyes, darkened to the color of a rich, fine whiskey. He would do what no other man had ever dared. He would command her body. He would give her unparalleled rapture then take what he needed, what he wanted.

Hell yeah! Fuck me! Kate's mind screamed her wild, wicked desires. She would give back what he gave ten-fold. Taunt, tease, and drive him to the edge of reason. Her pussy clenched and proof of her desire slid down her crack. This man would match her lust for lust, need for need, and bring every fantasy to life.

Seductively she drew her fingers over her breasts, across her abdomen, and against her clit, which screamed for attention. "Do I have to take care of this myself? Are you not up to the challenge?"

Oh shit. You're in for it now, girl! His eyes turned even darker, hands clenched in fists at his sides. She'd provoked the bull and he was ready to charge. Good!

Jesse crawled up the bed between her spread legs. He looked powerful—a starving mountain lion about to feast on its latest kill. Shivers coursed through her body in response. Kate knew she was about to have on hell of an amazing time.

"Raise your arms above your head, and hold onto the headboard. Don't let go, Katie. I'll have to punish you if you do."

Punish her? Oh hell, now she'd really done it. Stepped in it right up to her eyes. Mmm...the very idea made her pussy weep.

Chapter Four

Jesse gave Kate everything she'd ever wanted and some things she hadn't realized were lacking in her past lovers. He was a grade-A prime, dominant alpha male, and she loved every wonderfully chauvinistic demand he made to ensure her enjoyment.

While she was an intelligent, competent, independent woman in business and life, in the bedroom she longed to surrender control. Give up all responsibility and bask in the glow of the one man strong enough to handle her needs. Somehow he'd recognized this secret compulsion smoldering below her cool exterior, and acted upon it.

Reaching up and holding the headboard as ordered caused her breasts to rise up deliciously. She rather fancied the effect as Jesse trailed his fingers over her calves then pushed her knees forward until they nearly bracketed her breasts, lifting her hips from the bed.

"Keep your legs right there. Don't move, honey."

She didn't even consider not obeying.

His fingers coasted along the inside of her thighs to her pulsing core and spread her outer lips. For long moments his intent gaze focused on her flesh.

"Jesse...please." She held the slats of the headboard in a white-knuckled grip.

"Not yet, honey." Jesse took his time to look at her before he lowered his head between her thighs, his silky hair tickling the sensitized flesh.

She needed his tongue on her clit with a viscous desperation. The cool brush of his breath over her sizzling flesh made Kate cry with incoherent mumblings. Time and place lost all meaning as she anticipated his first touch, knowing it wouldn't take much.

When it finally came, so did Kate.

His flattened out tongue glided up the length of her slit, then grazed over her quivering clit. That was all it took to send her flying. The hot, wet caress filled every muscle with tension before she exploded. He lapped up every drop of her response with greedy growls, refusing to let the tension ebb.

"Damn, you taste so sweet. Honey and raspberries. Exquisite."

Stiffening his tongue, Jesse circled her clit before moving lower to fuck her vagina. The walls of her channel pulsed as he tongued her, fast and energetic. One orgasm blended into another in an endless succession as Kate soared and dipped, flying higher and higher.

Jesse could spend hours eating her pretty pussy. Her addictive taste exploded in his mouth as he drank in her erotic essence. He loved the way Kate abandoned herself to his ministrations, surrendering so beautifully. Her hips bucked as she writhed, fucking his mouth. She cried, pleaded and moaned, giving it all to him, submitting to his passion.

He wasn't into the whole D/s lifestyle, even though it was the focus of his internet business. Jesse just loved nothing more than to have an assertive woman gift him with the power to control her body and her satisfaction in the bedroom. He didn't want some simpering plaything to torture and abuse—he wanted a partner willing to indulge their mutual desires. The woman convulsing under his tongue was everything he wanted, needed.

He mercilessly drove her from one shattering peak to another, again and again, not staying in any one spot too long. Her thighs trembled weakly, yet she kept her legs where he'd instructed. Jesse knew her hands longed to sink into his hair, hold his head where she wanted, but she held firm to the headboard.

"Good girl!"

While he continued to lick, suck, and nip, Jesse thrust three fingers into her pussy. He stroked her G-spot with a come-hither motion that drove her crazy. He didn't slow down until she no longer had the strength to hold her legs, and had collapsed into a sated heap.

Aftershocks still pulsing through her pussy, Jesse rose from the bed. He quickly found a rubber in his jeans pocket, ripped open the packet, and rolled the sheath over his rock hard shaft. Kneeling between her legs, he lifted her pelvis and placed two pillows under her hips, angling her for the deepest possible penetration.

"Open your eyes, Katie."

Her head thrashed from side to side, but her eyes remained stubbornly shut. Jesse deepened his voice, making it more authoritative, and repeated the order. He pressed the tip of his cock against her wet hole, and her eyes sprung wide open.

"Keep those pretty eyes open, Red. I want to see them while I fuck you hard. Want you to see me."

Kate whimpered, but maintained eye contact. Satisfied, he drove his cock into her with one fluid thrust. She cried out, expressing delight over how completely he filled her.

"You're so tight...hot...wet," he praised.

He held still as a statue, allowing her to adjust, savoring the moment. However, she wasn't content with holding still. She began to wiggle beneath him, trying to get him to move until his stern voice halted her frantic attempts.

"Don't move or I'll pull out!"

"No. God, no!"

He couldn't, he wouldn't, but she didn't know that. He was testing her to see if she could truly give up control, submit to his will. Didn't matter if it was killing him, Jesse didn't move a muscle. Neither did she.

"Good girl!"

The arrogant comment rankled Kate's nerves. Who the hell did he think he was? Every stubborn bone in her body wanted to tell him to fuck off, kiss her lily white ass. She ruthlessly fought against the natural instinct. If she let loose some flippant response he'd leave her empty, which would surely drive her insane.

A self-satisfied smirk curled over his lips, while Kate clenched her jaw tight and fought her body's needs. Just when she was close to losing it, he pulled back until only the tip of his cock remained.

No! She wanted to scream. Would beg and plead, offer him the world—anything to bring his thick shaft back, get him to continue stretching her so wonderfully.

After what seemed hours, he began moving in a tortuous, slow rhythm, letting her feel every delicious inch slipping in and out, back and forth.

"Look at yourself, Katie. See how your pussy stretches around my cock, struggles to take more of me. Do you want the rest?"

The rest? There was more? How could she possibly take

more? He already stretched her beyond anything she could have ever imagined. Kate pulled on the headboard, lifting her shoulders until she could see the point where their bodies joined. His substantial shaft impaled her, forcing her tissues to accommodate his girth.

Wow! It was an unbelievable sight, but the feisty wench she'd kept in check finally burst loose, no longer willing to be kept under lock and key.

"Give me every inch. Fuck me hard with that big cock."

Holy cow, did those words just come out of my mouth?

She stared up at him, defiance burning in her eyes, unwilling to admit her limitations. If there was more, then she wanted it. She would make him give it to her one way or another. She wouldn't be denied or treated as something fragile.

He held her hips pinned to the pillows so she was unable to move. She still gripped the headboard tight. She trembled at the wicked look overtaking his features right before he drilled into her hard and fast, deeper than should be possible. Further than anyone else had ever gone.

Her mouth opened, but the scream strangled in her throat. The wet sound of their sweaty flesh slapping together filled her ears, which already pounded with her raging blood. Every driving thrust filled her to overflowing for mere seconds before he withdrew again, leaving her empty and bereft. It was an endless, maddening cycle.

The scent of their sex permeated her lungs. Every fiber of her being focused on the total fusing of their bodies. Tension built to unbearable levels, and the scream finally bubbled up from her throat as her world exploded in white-hot shards of light. Pure bliss surged from the roots of her hair to each rigid, curled toe.

Jesse gave her pleasure beyond belief. His cock continued

to jackhammer into her body as she convulsed, flooding them both with her come. Letting herself go, giving everything to this amazing man, she felt carefree and light.

When a second, no-less-exquisite orgasm rolled through her, Jesse's voice and motions became more and more distant. Darkness closed in at the edges of Kate's vision. Although she fought a brave fight to hang on to every sensation, the impossible swelling of his cock as it pounded into her pussy shattered her.

Jesse held off longer then he would have thought possible. When Kate's body surrendered to his, it was more than he could take. Lightening shot down his spine and gathered in his balls before exploding from the head of his cock in a stunning climax. Her pelvic muscles clamped down on his shaft, preventing further movement, absorbing his climax deep within her, drawing his life's essence from his body.

He collapsed over her, barely managing to get his arms under his chest so he wouldn't crush her beneath his weight. He couldn't move, couldn't breathe. Sweat poured off him, dripping down his face and into his eyes. He couldn't have cared less.

The sheer total stillness of the woman beneath him finally gave Jesse enough strength to roll to his side. He stared into her slack, relaxed face before realizing what had happened. He'd not only fucked her senseless, he'd fucked her unconscious.

Holy shit!

After prying her fingers from the headboard slats, Jesse curled his body around Kate in a protective manner. Gut-wrenching tenderness and awe filled him. She was everything he'd ever wanted, and more than he'd ever dreamed of finding.

His fingers traced the angles of her beautiful face. There

would be no turning back. She was his now. Claimed by him, fucked by him, owned by him. They'd be together come hell or high water.

When he was finally able to move again, Jesse threw away the spent condom and took a shower. His cock returned to semi-hardness as her scent enveloped him while washing with her soap. After drying off, he found a basin under the sink and filled it with warm, soapy water. Slow and tender, he tended to her body while she slept.

Jesse got dressed and walked back to his apartment, leaving her only briefly. He'd rushed out the door so fast he hadn't even locked up. While cleaning his ejaculate off the glass doors, he watched over Kate.

After securing his place, he returned to her bed, stripped and climbed in beside her. Kate barely stirred as he spooned close against her back, pulling the covers over them both. She was exhausted and needed to rest, but Jesse needed back inside. He slowly worked his semi-erect cock into her still wet pussy, and sighed in contentment.

It felt magnificent to be sheathed in her body without any barriers between them. Never before had he been inside a woman without latex separating their flesh. Kate was different. She was his woman, and he didn't want anything to come between them again. He wanted to enjoy the hot clasp of her body as they slept.

Somehow he would find a way to convince Kate to come to the ranch with him. He knew she was the woman for him, and wanted to introduce her to his friends and ranch life. The situation may be uncomfortable until he built his house, what with Tamara so close by, but she had Dakota.

The idea of sharing Kate with his friends held a certain appeal. He understood why Cord had shared Savannah with the ranch hands. While Jesse would enjoy giving Kate so much sexual ecstasy, he just didn't think he'd be able to handle watching anyone else touch her. She belonged to him, and only him. He felt incredibly selfish when it came to her.

Jesse fell into a comfortable sleep with his cock buried in the beautiful woman he already loved. The feelings had built up over the past few weeks and become cemented tonight when she'd proven to be his dream girl. He wouldn't deny it for a moment. He was completely and helplessly head-over-heels.

ℰℴ

If the shrill beeping of the alarm clock had not dragged Kate out of sleep, the masculine grunt, followed by a large arm stretching across her body sure would have succeeded.

Vivid images, scents, tastes, sounds, and touches from the night flowed through her memory. From the solid mass still next to her, Kate knew Jesse had stayed all night.

Oh, what a night!

Her body was sore and achy in numerous places. The cowboy was one hell of a demanding lover. But, boy oh boy, he gave back even more than he took.

Unfortunately, she didn't have time for wake-up sex. If she did not get moving there was no way she'd make it to work on time. And the last thing she wanted was to give D.H. a reason to ride her ass all day.

She loved her work. Being a graphic artist had been Kate's dream. The recognition she'd received for her art gave her an incredible feeling of pride. Several of her designs had won prestigious awards. No, her work wasn't the problem, her boss was. D.H. did everything within his power to knock her down.

Kate and Tink were sure it was due to the weasel being intimidated by her confidence and abilities.

If it wasn't for Tink working with her at Riesman Designs, Kate would have left long ago. But she needed the job and the experience. If she ever hoped to start her own business, she had to continue saving up capital and make new business connections. She had the ambition, determination and drive to make it happen. She'd fought to prove herself, prayed D.H. would finally promote her. Some management experience under her belt, and Kate would be an unstoppable force rising all the way to the top.

She loved everything about working in the competitive design field. Power lunches and suits, high-pressure meetings, prestigious awards and accolades. Running her own firm, her own way, holding all the power... Damn, she could almost taste it.

As Kate tried to climb out of the bed, Jesse's arm tightened around her waist, pulling her in to a solid wall of muscle. His morning erection pressed up against her hip. Very tempting, but work beckoned.

Great! How was she supposed to get one very large, horny cowboy out of her apartment in order to get ready for work? Even if she managed to wiggle out of his tight grasp, Kate wasn't about to leave him sleeping in her bed.

She took a fortifying breath. *Okay, you can do this.*

Attempting to lift his arm was similar to trying to bench press her own weight. It took a while, but she managed to wriggle out from under the beefy appendage. She'd just swung her legs out of the bed when his grumbling voice stopped her cold.

"Just where do you think you're going?"

She turned and gave him her most serious, intimidating

glare. The one which made her competition cringe. It didn't seem to have much impact on Jesse, though. "Look, cowboy. It was fun, but I've got things to do. I have a life, a career. If I don't get moving, I'll be late. So um...it's time for you to go."

His rumbling laughter was the last thing Kate had expected. Did he think she was making some kind of joke?

"Nice try, honey. You can't get rid of me that easily."

Well, his statement sure put the starch in her backbone. Kate straightened to her full height, and defiantly lifted her chin.

"Now, don't go gettin' your panties in a bunch. We just need to get a few things straight first." He lazily stretched across her bed. "Then you can go."

The casual comment telling her what she would do chapped her ass. Of all the nerve. The arrogant SOB. Who the hell did he think he was? No one treated her as inferior and got away with it. Anger and frustration rose. Kate balled her hands into tight fists at her sides. She felt her blood pressure skyrocket, heat filling her face and neck.

"I *might* be willing to talk to you later, but right now, you need to leave."

Those smoldering eyes darkened dangerously. Jesse held her immobile with his fierce gaze. "Look, honey..."

Okay, that did it!

"Don't *honey* me. This is my apartment, and I asked you to leave. If you are not gone by the time I get out of the shower, I'm calling the police."

Jesse's laughter rang through the room, pissing her off. She strove so hard to look in charge and menacing. She couldn't really bully the huge cowboy who could subdue her without breaking a sweat. At least the tactic worked with D.H., but he was spineless.

"Oh hell, honey. You sure got some balls. Just don't try to push me too far." His voice took on the commanding tone which turned her on. "We'll discuss this after I've had some coffee."

In one smooth movement, he dropped his legs over the side of the bed and stood to his full height. Kate was not able to stop herself from flinching, then taking a step backwards. She didn't think he'd actually hurt her, but what did she know about him? Next to nothing.

She tried to take a deep breath, but it burned her lungs. Anger twisted her stomach into a tight knot, sending icy chills through her body. While it was okay, even desirable for a man to be dominating and take control in bed, it was not okay for him to think he could dictate and control her life.

With calculated movements, Jesse gathered up his clothes and leisurely dressed. She was surprised he let her pass by and move into the bathroom without comment. She prayed he'd be gone by the time she was finished.

Chapter Five

Even the cold shower had not managed to take the heat out of Kate's temper. Her foul mood radiated from her body like a bad odor, infecting everyone and everything she touched.

She understood why she was angry. She craved Jesse. He satisfied her sexually and touched her heart. He made her mind wander to things she'd given up for her career. Things like marriage and family. Things that didn't fit into her life anymore and only served to distract Kate from her plans. That scared her, and she hated feeling that way. In fact, it pissed her off.

Finding the note—actually they were orders—Jesse left on her kitchen table had nearly burst a blood vessel in her head. The sharp, searing pain still stabbed through her temple and right eye. The arrogant jerk had stated in no uncertain terms that he would pick her up at seven o'clock for dinner, and she had better be ready or be prepared to face punishment.

Punishment. She wasn't some child he could boss around and send to her room. No other man had dared to treat Kate in such a manner. They groveled, begged, showered her with gifts. But to issue a command, then threaten punishment. Oh, if that cowboy knew what was good for him, he'd hightail it back to the ranch.

With savage aggression, Kate slammed her hand down on the horn and held it for several long moments. The loud irritating sound finally captured the attention of the stupid driver sitting through the green arrow just in time for him to squeal through the light, leaving her stuck waiting through another cycle.

"Fuck me!"

Well, no. She'd already been fucked, several times. That was certainly not what Kate needed.

She could feel the road rage bubbling up from some dark, angry place deep inside, but there was little Kate could do to prevent the backlash. Heaven help anyone who got in her way today. D.H. had better be on his best behavior.

Man, she should have stayed home in bed. There was no way she'd get any constructive work done in this frame of mind. She felt a momentary flash of pity for all the nice, normal people she would come into contact with today.

Kate could only hope the rage radiating off her would keep everyone at a distance. Lord knows she had no business being around anyone in her current state. Shit, she should be whistling, humming, full of happiness and joy after a night of the best sex known to womankind. But no, instead she was pissed off.

If she had been in a different frame of mind, Kate might have laughed at the look on the receptionist's face when she glowered at the woman. Norma's unnaturally sunny disposition was annoying at the best of times. Kate often wondered if the woman gave herself a liquid sunshine enema each day. It just wasn't normal to be so bright and perky when at work early in the morning.

"Good morning, Kate. I have some messages for you and an addition to your schedule."

She looked over the papers Norma handed her, noting the lunchtime appointment, and Kate's mood went even farther down the tubes.

"What the fuck. I don't get a lunch break now? This place sucks!"

Norma cringed, then sighed in relief when she was rescued by the ringing phone. Of course it wasn't Norma's fault that D.H. had scheduled an appointment for her to meet with a new client over lunch. It was the poor woman's misfortune D.H. was not around to face her wrath at that moment, resulting in her kill-the-messenger attitude.

She mumbled an apology and headed for her office.

Kate had just booted up her computer when Tink strolled in, talking a mile a minute about one of her new toys. While Kate enjoyed test driving toys for her friend's online sex shop, today wasn't a good day to discuss anything involving sex. The subject made her think about Jesse, which reignited her anger.

On top of the new client, she had a team project due in one of her current college classes. Working on her bachelor's degree and working full time in an attempt to get established in the graphic design business kept her busy. It was difficult to stay on top of it all, but she loved every second. And still, she demanded more from herself. For the past six months she'd been putting in extra hours helping Tink revamp her website. The sensual designs were some of Kate's best work ever, and made her very proud.

"Damn, girl. You are not going to believe all the things this new vibrator does. It has four speeds, and six different patterns of vibrations. It also has rotate and thrust settings. Damn thing does everything but bring you flowers. We won't even need men anymore."

Plopping down into the chair across from Kate's desk, Tink brushed her long blonde hair over a slim shoulder. When she paused in her constant prattle long enough to look at Kate's stony expression, she frowned.

"Who put the starch in your panties this morning?" Tink teased. "Ohhh, was it Tom the peeping cowboy? Damn, you still owe me details, girl."

Tink smiled, staring at Kate's neck. Talk about weird. Sometimes she didn't get her quirky friend. And right now Tink was getting on her last nerve. Wanting details of a private moment, one she had yet to sort out her confused feelings about, sparked irrational feelings within Kate.

"Damn it, Tink. I love you, but I'm in no mood for this today. Go find someone else to mess with for a while." Kate struggled to be calm. She didn't want to take out her frustration on her friend.

"Okay, bad subject. I'll, uh just leave this here. Come find me if you need to talk."

The nine inch long blue vibrator sat in the middle of Kate's in-basket. Tink smiled again, shook her head, then headed back to her cubicle.

Although the brush-off was sure to have stung, Tink would know she was venting. It was a sign of true friendship to be able to rant with your girlfriend while in a foul mood and laugh about it later. And they would laugh about everything once she calmed down. The two of them had been through similar scenes and hard words many times before.

Of course, now Tink would feel obligated to find some way of getting Kate out of her crappy mood. All morning the practical joke queen would plot her next move. Hopefully she'd save her antics for after work.

Putting an abrupt halt to the unproductive train of thought, Kate took a cleansing breath and settled into her work.

Bored almost to the point of tears with the know-it-all jerk rambling on endlessly, Jesse found his mind wandering to the very luscious Kate. A smile crept across his lips as he considered her probable reaction to the instructions he'd left.

His brief chuckle gave the idiot speaking the impression he was actually responding to the incessant drivel. Oh well. Let the idiot get his hopes up. There was no way Jesse would employ the services of such an unimaginative bore. No, when he found the right person to help create the image he wanted for his business, he'd know it immediately.

Maybe the meeting he had scheduled to follow this one would be more promising. The man he'd spoken with this morning had claimed to have an award-winning artist who would have no problem bringing his vision to life. Damn, he sure hoped so.

Then he could go back to the ranch. Somehow he'd find a way to convince Red to come with him. They were perfect for each other. Whether she knew it or was willing to admit it to herself, Jesse felt it to be true.

Just thinking of the feisty fireball had his cock stiffening. She'd met him lust for lust, not once questioning anything he wanted or demanded. Letting all inhibitions go, Kate had responded with a passion he wouldn't turn away from. She'd tried to hide behind her temper this morning, but he wouldn't let her push him away. Maybe he'd bring her some flowers and turn that passion in a direction they'd both enjoy.

And by the time he showed up at her apartment tonight she should be good and ready for some action. Anticipation of the night to come sent shivers coursing down his spine.

෨

As she'd feared would happen, Kate had been unable to get any work done. One tall, dark and handsome cowboy kept invading her thoughts. He'd sure figured out how to push her buttons. Both the good and bad ones.

Her mind kept flashing back to the way he'd taken charge in bed, demanding she surrender to the extreme pleasure only he could provide. And had he ever provided. Wow! She was getting hot just remembering.

Jesse's huge cock had filled her so completely, fulfilling untold desires, bridging an unexpected void. Not only did he have the equipment, but the man knew what to do with it. Kate's nipples tightened as she recalled the mind-melting ecstasy. Hell, she'd even passed out.

She wanted to drop down on her knees and thank Tink for her interference. At the same time, Kate wanted to smack her friend for bringing this situation about. Of course, how could Tink have known what a total alpha male her peeping Tom would turn out to be?

The beep of the intercom pulled Kate from her thoughts seconds before sunshiny Norma spoke, grating on her already raw nerves.

"Um, Kate. I need you to come out to the lobby. There is a...um...gentleman here demanding to see you. Could you please come? Right now!"

Somehow Norma's voice did not sound quite right. It actually seemed to quiver and Kate detected a definite strain. No matter how irritating Norma's perpetual sunny disposition, Kate did not want to see something upset the woman.

"I'll be right there."

As she made her way down the hallway, she smoothed out her sleeveless black dress. While normally she liked to wear bright colors, the dark outfit suited her demeanor, seeming appropriate for the day.

Tink shot a questioning glance her way as Kate passed the other woman's desk. She just shrugged her shoulders in response to the silent question.

She approached Norma's desk from a hallway which came into the lobby at a right angle. She wasn't able to see into the waiting room, and didn't even glance in that direction. The distressed look on the receptionist's face had captured and held Kate's attention.

"What's wrong, Norma? I'm very busy preparing from my lunchtime meeting." The words came off sounding impatient and bothered, but Kate was actually concerned.

The poor woman was apparently too flustered to speak. She just pointed into the waiting area.

Kate turned sharply on her four-inch heels and nearly face-planted on the marble floor. Before her stood a nearly naked man wearing some wicked, black leather BDSM outfit with five straps buckled across his chest, a large silver ring in the center. He also wore a thick black collar with metal studs and ring dangling down over his throat, an attached leash draped over one shoulder.

What the fuck? Halloween was more than a month away.

Skimpy leather bikini underpants, which barely covered his manhood, were attached to one of the straps. Heavy black boots covered what appeared to be small feet. A pair of thick shackles held his wrists firmly together. He looked both cold and frightened. Kate merely stared, unable to find any words to address him or sort this mess out.

He stood a few inches shorter than her and had the trim, compact body of a runner. Sandy blond hair hung over his eyes, giving him a diminutive look. Overall not unattractive, but he needed a different outfit and some confidence.

Jesus, she'd been thrown into a bondage-gone-wrong nightmare. What the hell was going on? As she stood pondering this unusual development, the man dropped to his knees before Kate. His gaze was downcast, restrained wrists held up toward her.

"Please, Mistress Kate. I promise not to misbehave again. Please don't leave me shackled any longer."

Kate stared at the strange man with her jaw hanging open practically to the floor. She didn't even notice the person walking into the lobby until he threw back his head and began laughing. The sound held a familiar note, but she had other issues to deal with. One man and one distressing situation at a time.

The newcomer was most likely her noon appointment arriving early. It was par for the course with the way the day was going, to have a new potential client show up in the middle of this bizarre scene.

Norma of Sunnybrook farms chimed in helpfully behind Kate. "Should I call the police, Miss Brooks?"

Kate rolled her eyes as shock transformed to irritation. She knew instinctively who held the keys to those shackles. The conniving witch had to be somewhere close, watching her warped joke play out.

Okay, first Norma, then Mr. Submissive, and finally the client. She'd deal with them one at a time.

Still staring at the ceiling, Kate took control of the situation. "No, Norma. That won't be necessary. Just find Tink. I'm sure she knows this *gentleman*, and will be in possession of the keys for his cuffs."

Once again she looked down at the man groveling at her feet. He was unable to completely suppress the smile curling up the corner of his mouth.

"You can get up now. The joke's over." Reaching out, she lent a hand to steady him as he rose. "Nice acting job, by the way."

Turning to face the client, Kate received another major shock. While handsome beyond words in his casual clothes, dressed in a tailored charcoal grey suit, black silk shirt and grey tie, Jesse Powers was devastating. He looked every inch the powerful businessman.

No sooner had Norma finished paging Tink over the intercom than the smart-ass prankster appeared from the darkened conference room to the left of the lobby. Tears were rolling down her face as she tried to walk, doubled over, arms clasped over her belly. Sharp peals of laughter followed her slow progression across the room, echoing off the walls.

Kate snapped at her friend. "Tink, you crazy bitch! So help me God, if you don't get your bondage buddy out of here before D.H. finds out..."

"He'll be stuck on that conference call for hours."

"Too late, things got cut short and he already knows," Norma warned in a low voice.

Dropping her face into her hands, Kate shook her head. *Absofuckinglutley wonderful.* There was going to be hell to pay now. D.H. was not about to let this one go without someone losing their job. Tink had gone way too far this time. Her intentions of cheering Kate up were good, but the results were going to suck.

"One of you *ladies* better have a good explanation as to why there is a half-dressed, handcuffed man in my lobby, and a new client watching your depraved activities," Barry Riesman, better known as D.H., bellowed

Prepared to make the ultimate sacrifice and bite the bullet, Kate turned to face her boss and claim responsibility for the unacceptable breech of office decorum. It didn't matter she was the hapless victim of the joke, she'd take the fall to save her well-meaning friend.

She stood tall, looking him in the eye, resigned to her fate. And looking him in the eye was the least disgusting place to settle her gaze. Instead of accepting his baldness, D.H. instead did an oily version of a comb-over. He had a pasty complexion, and was pathetically out of shape. The way his fat belly rolled over the top of his belt was beyond gross.

"Well, you see, Mr. Riesman..."

Jesse's deep baritone cut her off, drowning out her voice, stopping the words that would have sent her to the unemployment line and killed her career. He boldly stepped forward, true to his dominant nature, and took control of the sinking ship.

Kate experienced a brief moment of déjà vu. Her hot cowboy neighbor sure seemed to have a thing about being in control. Somehow he managed effortlessly to do so in every situation. She'd have to think about it, but later. Now wasn't the time.

"Hello, Barry. I'm Jesse Powers. I do believe that I mentioned the somewhat controversial nature of my business when we spoke this morning. I felt a small display would allow your artist to get a better feel for what I'm trying to accomplish. Please excuse the rather unorthodox manner in which I chose to do so."

Extending his hand, Jesse eclipsed D.H.'s hand in a firm grasp. She watched as Jesse clapped his hand on the smaller man's back, and turned him around, heading toward Barry's office. Taking on a good ol' boy attitude, using his air of command, Jesse wound her pain-in-the-ass boss around his finger with ease.

"Sorry if I disrupted the work flow," he chuckled. "I just love to see the look on a woman's face when confronted with an embarrassing situation." The last was spoken in a conspiratorial whisper.

The bastard. How did he do it? Within the space of a heartbeat, Jesse had the whole nightmare contained, boxed, and wrapped up nice and neat with a pretty bow on top. Thankfully, this time it worked in her favor.

What a master of manipulation. She'd be wise to remember the fact.

With a wink over his shoulder at Kate, Jesse gave Barry a punch on the arm, almost knocking the rotund man down. "You know how it is," he continued. "A man's gotta find a little fun where he can."

Barry laughed without any real humor in the choked sound. "Oh, um...sure. I understand, Mr. Powers. Not a problem at all. You sure pulled one over on those girls." The dickhead tried to sound like he was one of the boys, in on a great joke.

Ugh! Kate wanted to scream at the top of her lungs, but held herself in check. As soon as the men were out of earshot, hands fisted on her hips, she turned on Tink. "Jesus! What the hell were you thinking? If Jesse hadn't snowed D.H., I would have lost my job while trying to save yours."

All signs of humor had disappeared from her friend's face. As usual, Tink had not thought far enough into the future to consider the possible fallout from her actions. All she'd thought about was getting a good laugh. She knew Tink had done it for her, to end her funk, but it still didn't change what almost happened.

Kate glanced at the shivering man, still restrained and looking lost. "For crying out loud, get the cuffs off of him and give the poor man something to wear before he freezes in this sub-artic air conditioning."

Tink pulled a key from her pants pocket, following Kate's instructions. When finally free, the man began to rub the circulation back into his wrists.

"I'm sorry, Kate. I never imagined D.H. finding out. The conference call should have kept him occupied." In pure Tink dramatic fashion, she fanned her face. "Holy crap. Please tell me the stud client is your cowboy neighbor, Tom. He is one fine hunk of a man."

Kate groaned and covered her face with her hands. She should have stayed in bed this morning.

Chapter Six

Barely making it to the restroom, Kate slammed the door closed and took several deep breaths.

It really had been one of Tink's better pranks. How the heck she'd come up with that one was something Kate didn't want to dwell on, though. If D.H. hadn't walked in at that exact moment, Tink would most assuredly have been rolling on the floor laughing her fool ass off, having a good time at Kate's expense.

She had no idea who the man was, but he deserved an academy award for his acting. And Jesse. Wow. She had to hand it to him—the cowboy sure knew how to turn things the direction he wanted them to go.

The surprise of discovering he was the dreaded lunchtime appointment had been overshadowed by the relief she'd felt when he deftly took D.H. under his control, saving her job. Yet she also held a bit of anger over his coming into her domain and acting all dominant.

"Face it," she chastised her mirror image. "The man ties you up in knots."

Knots. Mmm...the thought brought to mind some of her darkest fantasies.

She groaned. "Get yourself together, woman."

After regaining her composure, Kate straightened her dress. While checking her make-up in the mirror, she spotted the love bite peeking out from her neckline.

"Shit," she gasped. "Thank goodness D.H. didn't notice." Her boss would have given her hell if he'd seen the mark. Why the hell hadn't Tink told her? It must be what she'd been staring at earlier.

Retrieving her make-up case from under the counter, she carefully applied concealer to the blemish. The purple mark stood out in bold contrast to her fair complexion. She retrieved an ivory cashmere sweater from her office as an extra precaution before joining D.H. to "meet" the potential new client.

It was readily apparent from the moment she walked through the door Jesse had successfully managed to snowball Barry. They were acting like two high school buddies reliving the glory days.

Ugh...men!

"Ah, right on time, Kate. Mr. Powers is ready to discuss his vision and hear some of your initial ideas."

Dismissing her just as quickly, D.H. turned back to Jesse. "Please, let me know if there is anything you need. As soon as lunch arrives, I'll have it brought into Kate's office. She'll be able to provide detailed information concerning our services."

Jesse nodded. "Thanks, Barry. I'm sure Miss Brooks will be able to take care of my needs."

A knowing, private smile crossed his lips and he shot her a lecherous look. The suggestive glance promised carnal delights beyond belief. And she knew he could deliver on what those sexy dimples implied.

Damn, he was good. With barely a glance or word, heat spread through her body. Little shivers of anticipation stretched outward from her core, which was headed towards a thermonuclear meltdown already.

Unable to reply, Kate turned and walked toward her office. She had no doubt Jesse would be close on her heels so she didn't bother to look back.

When the door closed behind them, his way-too-large form seemed to crowd what she had considered a comfortable, roomy space. Somehow her office now felt small and cramped as he filled the room. His natural masculine scent inundated her senses, and her body thrummed with unfulfilled need. Images from their night together once again flashed through her mind, complete with sounds, tastes, textures, and warmth.

The man was lethal.

She loved the way his eyes darkened with carnal lust, the heavy-lidded gaze making her feel boneless. She wanted to melt into his body, relax and let him take control.

Giving herself a mental slap, Kate squared her shoulders and prepared for battle. What the heck kind of spell was he putting her under? She did not relinquish control to anyone. Kate Brooks ruled the business world. This was her office, and she was in command. Right?

Pushing away thoughts of relaxing for once and letting someone else take the reins, Kate glared at her adversary.

"Just what did you think you were doing taking blame for the scene out front? You had nothing to do with Tink's joke. And what kind of business can possibly justify such a scene to D.H.'s satisfaction?"

Kate paused briefly to take a calming breath. Another, very pertinent question occurred to her. "Oh, and another thing. What the hell are you doing here? Did you follow me to work?"

Jesse's heated gaze continued to melt her insides. Instead of responding, he slowly moved closer, looking every inch the wild beast stalking its prey. He invaded her personal space, crowding her between his overwhelming presence and the desk. His body was so close it was all she could see, all she could smell.

Kate wanted to dive right in, indulge in a little afternoon delight. The sinful man was hell on her restraint!

Jesse had glanced around the office, learning a great deal about Red in those few seconds. Everything was streamlined, neat and well-ordered. The space was organized to the extreme and reflected a woman used to being in command.

No stray papers littered the spotless desk top. Not even a pen lay on the blotter. There were no feminine personal touches. Everything was businesslike and proper.

The short time he'd had to observe told him Kate was one high-strung, wound tight, large-and-in-charge power player in desperate needed of letting go. He was going to enjoy taking control of her body, training her to please him and ruffling her feathers a bit.

Stalking her every movement, he kept going until she backed into the desk. "I'm here because I need a skilled graphic artist. And yes, I took over things out there because I didn't want to see you lose your job over your co-worker's joke. Got a problem with that?"

God, being so close to her lush body had the blood leaving his brain and heading south. How was he supposed to think about business while her clean feminine scent washed over him?

Something else flickered along the edges of his consciousness. There was something Barry had said which bothered him. "Why does Riesman have the impression you're his plaything? Do you have something going with your boss?

Tell me you're not sleeping with him!"

If she was having an affair with the pompous ass, Jesse didn't know how he'd handle it, but was certain his response wouldn't be pretty. He was feeling very possessive of *his* sly red fox. There was no way he'd share her with the oily little creep.

Kate's heartfelt laughter sank deep into his soul. Thankfully, the spirited woman seemed to have no idea how far she'd gotten under his thick skin or her devastating impact on him.

"Sleep with D.H.? That's a good one. Although he's made things crystal clear. Fucking him would benefit my career at Riesman Designs, but no thanks! I'd rather not succeed if the cost is letting him touch me."

Dark rage spread though his entire body. He'd kill the disgusting pervert. Ring the very life from his round body.

"It's okay, Jesse. I can handle D.H." Kate's words caressed his soul as her soft fingers caressed his cheek.

A wicked smile spread across his lips as he noticed the large blue vibrator so blatantly out of place sitting in her in-basket. In mere seconds an all encompassing need took over his every action and reaction. Sinful ideas of how to try out the device flooded his head.

"I think we need a little appetizer before lunch." The quick change of topic seemed to throw her off guard. Good.

He winked, and Kate's lungs seized, depriving her of much needed oxygen. Her head was spinning as she tried to keep up with what was happening. Jesse had her sandwiched between his powerful body and her desk with no escape route. She wanted to give in, sink into the comfort of his body, and not worry about anything. Would it really be so bad to let him take control, give up all responsibility to the very capable man who

69

stood too close? Wasn't it what she'd wanted for a long time?

Damn if those tempting, devilish dimples were not wreaking havoc on her hormones again. How was she supposed to resist such temptation? She wasn't strong enough.

He picked up the big blue vibrator, a bad-boy gleam in his scorching gaze. Crap, how had she managed to leave the damn vibe sitting out in the open like a hand-engraved invitation?

"All work and no play makes Katie a dull girl," he teased.

His gravelly voice was right next to her ear, breath heating her flesh. Shivers ran through her body in response to the sensual assault. This would not do.

Placing both palms flat against his chest, Katie had planned to push him away, but touching him had been a tactical mistake. His concentrated heat seared her hands, surging up her arms, firing her blood. Jesse's intent gaze was an intimate caress, bringing every nerve ending to life, causing a wet flow to erupt between her legs.

His eyes locked with hers and Kate was lost. Her lust-fogged brain barely registered the low humming sound before vibrations shocked her turgid nipple. Electric impulses spread through her breast and shot straight to her already throbbing clit.

"Get up on the desk."

His tone brooked no room for argument. Jesse expected her to do what he said, when he said it. Things were rapidly spiraling out of hand. Her focus narrowed to the two of them and the amazing things he'd do with the vibrator, which pissed her off.

They were in a place of business where she worked, and Jesse thought he'd charge in and turn her into a sex-starved slut. And here she was ready to give in. Kate hated herself for the power she'd given him. She'd handed him the keys to her soul on a silver platter by letting him see how much she loved his dominance in bed last night.

"Don't you dare go assuming you can barge into my home, have sex with me, and then I'm yours to order around. Well, not here, caveman. And not now."

There was his spirited woman, showing her temper and claws. Jesse found her even more enticing when she got all fierce and sassy. After all, a good challenge was half the fun, and he was up for the task in a very literal way. A bit of fight made for stimulating foreplay.

He knew when to keep quiet. Instead of fighting back with words, Jesse dove headfirst into an all out sensual assault. With a tap of his finger, the vibrations increased and he began teasing the other nipple poking through her dress, begging for attention.

Kate's back arched as she sought more pressure. Jesse held back a triumphant grin. He hadn't won the battle yet, but was pleased with how things were going. Before long, she would be begging him to do whatever he wanted with her luscious body.

"Take off the sweater, honey."

Kate blinked her glassy eyes then shrugged out of the garment and let it fall in a heap on the desk. The vibrator was trapped between their bodies as he reached behind her and unzipped the dress then slid the straps down her arms.

White silk and lace hugged her breasts and disappeared beneath the waistline of her dress. It was becoming obvious she had a thing for erotic lingerie and damn if it didn't turn him on. His cock stiffened, pressing against the confinement of his pants as he wondered about the rest of the outfit. Would it be as devastating?

There were no two ways about it. He had to see what his temptress was wearing, but he also had to consider where they were and her job.

"Is there a lock on the door, Kate?"

She seemed confused, staring at him as he continued to run the vibrator around her nipples. Removing the distraction, he pulled the blue device away from her body. When she would have protested, he asked the question again.

"Yes."

"Good girl. I want you to go lock the door, then take the dress off."

Some of the desire left her eyes, replaced by defiance and the lively spirit which was part of what he loved about her. Kate looked around and her cheeks heated. Crossing her arms over her chest, she said, "Not here."

The words, combined with her rebellious stance, boiled his blood and tightened his balls. If she knew how that bold, saucy attitude affected him, Jesse doubted she'd be making a stand.

"Do you want to be spanked, because that's where you're headed, honey."

He watched as her eyes heated with lust and indecision played across her features.

"Fine, have it your way. Turn around, hold onto the desk, and accept your punishment."

Instead, Kate shifted to the side and quickly moved around the desk. She walked backward, keeping her gaze on his as she locked the door. Standing in the middle of her office, she shimmied her hips until the dress dropped down around her ankles.

The view was even better than he'd anticipated. The skimpy teddy molded to every curve, flared high over her hips and narrowed to a thin strip of silk covering her mound. Each breathless rise and fall of her chest let him know how much she rejoiced in his dominance. Kate needed this, needed him, to remove her self-imposed constraints.

"Come here, Katie."

She sucked her lower lip into her mouth and bit into the tender flesh with her teeth. A fierce battle was being waged between her need for discipline and her desire to let go. Her desires won, and she slowly moved back between his body and the desk.

Pride and elation made him want to shout, but Jesse held himself in check. This was about Kate and her pleasure.

"Good girl." From the look which crossed her face, Jesse knew the words rankled, but she remained quiet.

"Turn around and put your hands on the desk, honey."

It was his turn to gasp when she did as instructed. There wasn't much to the back of the teddy. Her perfect round ass was completely exposed except for a tiny strap disappearing down the crevice between the cheeks.

"I love your taste in underwear. Damn, Katie. You're killing me."

Killing him? He had to be joking. Kate had no willpower or resistance where Jesse Powers was concerned. The man fogged her mind worse than a fine wine rushing straight to her head. One command spoken in his dark velvet voice and she came to heel. A well-trained puppy, ready to please her master. One touch and the savvy business woman went right out the window.

Holy crap. She was bent over her desk in nothing but a teddy while he stood behind her fully dressed and holding a vibrator. She didn't know what to expect. Simply contemplating his next move made her wet. There was some innate quality in

Jesse which made her trust the cowboy and allowed her to relax.

She started when his hand gathered her hair and moved the thick mass over her shoulder. Goose bumps broke out over her skin as his calloused fingers caressed her bare back. Her inner thighs were slick with her arousal. She fought the urge to wriggle and press her legs together to relieve the ache.

His hands tickled over her ass with a feather-light touch one moment, then landed a stinging slap which made her squeal in surprise the next. He soothed away the slight pain and Kate whimpered. Jesse was moving so slow. She needed him to fuck her right here and right now. Split her open with his beautiful cock and make her scream.

"Jesse...please!"

Several sharp smacks landed in quick succession, heating her flesh. Kate began to squirm, raising her ass for each blow, falling into his rhythm.

"I'll please you, honey, once you tell me who owns this ass."

Oh, hell no. Did he really expect her to say something so degrading?

Before she uttered a word, he began to spank her again. Hard. Intense heat built in her abused flesh and she loved it. The mere idea of deriving enjoyment from being spanked should have had her running for the door instead of making her nipples tingle and her pussy gush.

"That's for even thinking of defying me." His hands caressed her cheeks, spreading the fire through her body. "Now tell me, Kate. Who owns this fine ass?"

She was dying, burning alive, and there was only one thing capable of putting out the flames. Kate was ready to do whatever it took to get what she wanted—his hard cock slamming into her dripping wet pussy.

"You do." The words weren't much more than a croaked whisper.

"Louder, honey. Tell me who's the only man that can provide what you need."

"Jesse. You own this body. Now hurry up and fuck me already."

His fingers stroked between her cheeks and circled her anus. "You're mine, honey. I'll fill this sweet ass." He continued to tease her tight pucker as pulled open the snaps between her legs, then slammed two fingers into her pussy. "And this tight cunt, when I'm ready."

Kate heard the devious grin in his response. The bastard wanted to make sure she knew he was in command, as if she could forget. She was very aware of who held the key to unlock her deepest desires and grant untold bliss.

She whimpered when his fingers slipped from her body, crying out as they were replaced with the dildo. He turned up the speed of the vibrations and set the device to gyrate. The combination sent her over the edge. There was no holding back the stunning orgasm. Every muscle tightened and the walls of her pussy began to spasm.

He kept thrusting the vibrator and rimming her anus, not letting Kate come down from the incredible high. When he let go of the blue wonder, the brutal contractions, along with the vibrators weight, pushed it from her body and onto the floor.

Jesse had to get inside her before he shot off in his pants like an untried teenager. He fumbled with his belt, ripped open his slacks, and took his aching cock in hand. Quick as a flash, he donned a rubber. Pushing against her back, Jesse exerted constant pressure until Kate's breasts flattened against the desk. With one hard thrust of his hips, he drilled into her welcoming flesh.

Oh, fuck! Her pussy spasmed and her hips bucked frantically. This was not going to last long. He pounded into her and reached around to stroke her engorged pearl.

It was too good. Jesse slammed into her until his balls tightened painfully and his come streaked through his cock. Molding his body to hers, he took her mouth in a possessive kiss, swallowing her cries when she came.

They rested against the desk while their bodies came down and their breathing evened out. He smiled and kissed the curve of her shoulder. Their bodies were damp with sweat, hair mussed, and the air reeked of sex.

A damn fine way to spend the afternoon as far as he was concerned.

Jesse didn't want to move, but they needed to clean up and get down to the actual reason for his being there—business. He groaned when his cock slipped from her damp heat then landed a playful slap on her ass.

"Get dressed, honey. We've got business to discuss."

Chapter Seven

Discombobulated was the best word Kate could come up with to describe her current state. Jesus, the crazy-ass cowboy had overwhelmed her judgment. He was dangerous. They'd had sex at the office, in her office, on top of her desk.

Holy shit! Another fantasy fulfilled.

All Jesse had to do was speak in his commanding voice, touch her, and everything else faded away. They could've been standing in the middle of a crowded shopping center and it wouldn't have fazed her. That was unacceptable. Frightening. She always maintained such rigid self-control.

She watched him drop the used condom in her waste basket, tuck in his shirt and zip up his pants as she scrambled to collect her clothes. No amount of smoothing out the crumpled dress with her hands was going to make a difference, and finger combing her hair probably only made the tussled tresses worse.

One look at her and everyone in the building would know what they'd been up to. Meanwhile the jerk looked no worse for the wear, damn him. It wasn't fair.

Kate did her best to set her desk back to rights, straightening the blotter and scooping up the spilled cup of pens. Her stapler was on the floor and she had no idea where her business card holder had ended up.

"Here's your day planner." The cheeky bastard smiled as he handed her the leather-bound book.

Her hand shook as she unlocked the door. It pissed her off that Jesse was able to command her body with such ease, slipping past her well-ordered and contained exterior to the wild, hidden submissive.

No sooner had she sat down behind the desk than Norma was at the door with lunch. A minute earlier and she would have caught them in the act. Kate wiped her damp brow. That was a little too close for comfort. What if D.H. had come to check on their progress? She shuddered at the thought.

Jesse moved into work mode smooth as silk. Hell, she practically had whiplash from the sudden change in demeanor. Dominant sex fiend one moment, composed businessman the next.

She pulled herself together while they ate lunch, then listened to him talk with intense passion about his business and what he hoped to accomplish. Kate took notes as her imagination provided vivid images of what he described.

"Being a dominant lover, even though I don't live the D/s lifestyle, I sought out others with similar interests on the internet. I found various chat rooms, and sites with information on the D/s lifestyle, but most were lacking. I wanted to learn more, and help others. This led to my idea for the creation of a safe, friendly community for those interested in the topic to find out more. A place where Doms and subs, whether lifestylers or not, can discuss a variety of topics, share techniques and ideas. It's also a place for like-minded people to come together and possibly make a connection."

Through his website, members were given access to legitimate merchants carrying bondage and training merchandise, as well as toys and other products of interest.

Kate made a note to have Tink discuss adding a link to her online toy shop to his listings.

"I maintain both monitored and private chat rooms, along with providing a customized version of dating services. With a lot of work, I've established a complicated screening process to help those with similar desires find one another. It even allows members to upload private video interviews for potential dates to view."

He detailed the intensive work his friend Stephanie had put into the website's various databases and functions. Kate suffered through a bout of jealousy as he talked with obvious affection about the other woman but Jesse was here with her, not off with Stephanie. The knowledge let Kate tamp down the useless emotion and concentrate on what he was saying once again.

"I want bold but tasteful colors and graphics, along with photos to match each page of the site. For example, on the punishment page, a picture of a bound sub being paddled. Her ass cheeks pink and warm thrust up toward the camera. One member is a photographer, and has made an extensive collection of artistic photos available. I've picked out several to be used in the designs."

He removed a flash drive from his jacket pocket and handed it across the desk. Kate uploaded the images onto her computer then returned the small storage device to Jesse.

They talked for more than an hour, and her mind swirled with ideas. She did a few quick, basic pencil drawings he seemed to like, and their discussion spurred other possibilities for them to consider. By the time Jesse left her office, Kate was eager to get to work.

He'd given her a guest account so she logged on to his website, Mastering Life. She found it to be a classy, tastefully done enterprise. Those she encountered in the public chat rooms sang the praises of the services provided and referred to Jesse as Master J.

Kate was sure her cheeks were bright pink when she accessed some of the archived articles on training, punishment, discipline...and good Lord, cock and ball torture.

"Tink," she called out when her friend walked down the hallway. "C'mere. You've gotta see this."

"Wuz up."

Kate's leg was bouncing with all the restless energy vibrating through her body. When Tink got an eyeful of the erotic pictures, the woman began muttering creative curses. Kate read the introductory information on Shibari as her friend studied the images.

"Bondage erotic arts are about pleasure, not pain. Two consenting adults playing, not S&M. The bottom is not merely restrained or immobilized, but derives gratification from the strain and pressure of ropes tied to squeeze the breasts and genitals." Kate paused in her reading. "What's a bottom?"

Tink laughed at her, the bitch. "Don't you know anything? Sheesh! A bottom is the sub. A top is the Dom."

Oh, okay. That made a certain kind of sense.

"Shibari uses intricate and aesthetically pleasing patterns crafted from several thin pieces of rope. The psychological impact of being bound is heightened by the use of asymmetric positions."

Many of the high-quality photographs they browsed were suitable to be on display in an art exhibit. The black and white ones were beautiful. The use of light, shadow and contrasts appealed to her own inner-artist, but the thought of being tied in such a manner left her cold. The extreme form of bondage was not for her.

80

"This site is fabulous. Do you think there's any chance of getting the peeping cowboy to include a link for The Vibratorium?"

The name of Tink's online toy shop always made Kate smile and triggered a Pavlovian response. Her skin heated as she pictured the large box containing all the toys she'd tested for Tink. It was stashed under her bed, awaiting her return home.

Of course, who needed a toy box with Jesse around? He was better than any battery-operated-boyfriend she'd ever encountered. Kate wondered if she'd finally found a man trustworthy enough to experiment in anal sex with. Countless botched trials with her long, thin vibrator had sadly left her yearning for more.

She adored anal stimulation and using toys there, but wasn't able to coordinate her efforts. The closer she got to orgasm, the less she was able to manage her movements. Her hands would become shaky, and she'd wind up frustrated.

Tink's hand flashed before her face, pulling Kate from her private musings.

"Hello. Earth to Kate. The lights are on. Is anyone home?"

Swatting away her friend's hand, Kate tamped down her rising arousal and tried to focus on the here and now.

"We still on for Mexican night?"

Now there was a weekly tradition she wasn't about to miss. Coronas, chips and spicy salsa, quesadillas...

"Hell, yes! I went grocery shopping yesterday so we're all set for tonight."

"Awesome, I'll be over at six. My new bikini was delivered yesterday and I can't wait to try it out. Right now I've got to go lock myself in the ladies room for a while, though. Those pictures made me hornier than a sailor on shore leave after six sexless months at sea."

Kate shook her head and chuckled as Tink sauntered out the door. Mexican night was something she was looking forward to. She needed a chance to decompress. Hanging out at the pool with her friends was just the ticket.

ℰↃ

Clad in skimpy string bikinis, Kate and Tink headed out to the pool nestled in the courtyard of the apartment complex. They carted several plates and bowls, along with a cooler and towels.

They were greeted by friendly shouts of hello and flirty whistles of appreciation from other residents who congregated to socialize with neighbors on warm evenings. A popular dance tune played on a portable radio as everyone relaxed after a long work week.

"Looking good, ladies," one hunky neighbor called out. This was followed by several hoots from other men and groans from the women. It was all good natured fun and wonderful stress relief.

After setting their things down on a table, Tink opened a couple of beers, popped a slice of lime in each, and they joined an ongoing conversation speculating on the newest resident. All the single women were worked up over the thirty-something, hunky doctor.

"If he's a gynecologist, I'll gladly let him examine me," one woman joked and it was the guys turn to groan.

Another woman chimed in with what she knew. "I heard he's actually some kind of lab research geek."

The easy conversation flowed through a variety of topics. A

few automated lights came on when the sun set. Still, much of the area remained in shadow and created a soothing, romantic setting.

After snacking on the treats they'd brought and talking for a while, Kate slipped into the inviting water, enjoying the cool caress against her skin. Since the underwater light had burned out a week previous, the pool was dark and had an intimate feel. She lounged on the steps with a cold beer resting on the deck and watched Tink do one of the things she did best—flirt.

Mike was rubbing Tink's shoulders while she teased Shane by dragging her fingernails up and down his chest. Bret dove into the pool and swam over to join the group. He sat on the steps near Kate, pulled her legs onto his lap and began massaging her feet. His strong fingers pressing into her tired flesh were heaven.

Kate laid her head back against the lip of the pool, luxuriating in the moment until one of the guys suggested, "Why don't we move this party inside?" Her entire body tensed and she prayed Tink wouldn't be crazy enough to accept the invitation.

"This *party* isn't going anywhere."

Jesse's deep, menacing voice reached out from the darkness and sent shivers down her spine. Kate jerked her feet free of Bret's hands, which had begun to wander toward her calves.

"We were supposed to meet at your apartment almost two hours ago," Jesse grumbled as he moved into a shaft of light.

Oh shit. His jaw was clenched, hands fisted at his sides.

She'd forgotten all about the infuriating note. Her calm washed away, replaced by the anger she'd felt earlier. Had it really only been a day they'd known each other? So much had happened in the short time that it seemed much longer in some ways.

"You mean the orders you left. Sorry, cowboy. I don't follow commands very well."

Kate's snippy attitude pushed Jesse's buttons. She had no right to be mad. She wasn't the one who had been stood up. And to find her wearing barely a scrap of cloth and letting some punk rub her legs... His temper was nearing its boiling point.

"We need to talk." The fire in his eyes sent the punk, along with the rest of the group, heading for higher ground. Several people left. Only Tink and two guys stayed around, wisely keeping their distance.

"I don't think so."

Just that quickly she dismissed him and swam off into the deep end. Well, she wouldn't make a clean getaway.

Jesse sat down on a chair and took his time slipping off his boots and socks. Then he shucked his shirt and jeans, thankful he'd worn boxers. He walked down the stairs, stood in the shallow end and dove into the crisp water, surfacing in the dark corner next to Kate. Moving in close, he trapped her between his body and the unyielding concrete.

"I said we need to talk."

"Look, Mr. Pushy. Spending one night together does not give you the right to order me around. I don't feel like talking to you."

He pressed in even closer until her breasts flatted against his chest. "Hmm...a full night and an afternoon delight should give me some kind of claim in my book."

Kate trembled, and her nipples turned to hard points poking into his muscles. Her mind may be fighting their attraction, but her body was ready and willing. Jesse traced a finger over her cheek. "We have unfinished business, honey."

He tipped her chin, tilted his head and fitted his mouth over hers, effectively cutting off any further conversation. Taking his time, he traced the plump curves with his tongue and nibbled her soft lower lip before deepening the kiss. Their tongues twisted and tangled, delved into every wet corner, tempted and tasted.

Kate might say she didn't want to talk, but her body softened for him, speaking a language in which he was fluent. She responded to his touch. Whether voluntary or involuntary was of little concern. Her fingers dug into his shoulders as Kate wiggled against him, encouraging a faster pace, but Jesse's mind was set on a slow seduction.

The weight of several interested glances pierced the darkness. Good, let them watch. Let them see who she belonged to, who had absolute command over her inviting body.

His hands flowed sinuously over each wet curve and valley, reminding him of the way rain rolled over the slick rock of the mountains back home. His gut clenched at the thought of the Shooting Star Ranch. Being with Kate lessened the ache to be back there, but created a new longing to share the peace of the beautiful land he loved with her. A tiny voice whispered through his mind insisting she'd thrive on the ranch.

Somehow he'd find a way to get her there. One trip to his home and she'd be hooked.

Kate broke the kiss and nuzzled his cheek. "Let's go upstairs, cowboy."

He let his slick fingers wander over her ribs and traced the fleshy outer edge of her breast before slipping beneath the thin material attempting to cover the lush globe. When he flicked the harden peak of her nipple, she moaned and arched her back.

"Jesse…please!"

"Please what, Katie?"

"Take me inside and fuck me."

The fingers of his other hand toyed with the edge of her bottoms, then under the material to play in her damp curls. She was so hot and ready for him.

"I kinda like it right here, honey. We've got this private, dark corner to ourselves. I'm going to fuck you, right here and now, surrounded by your friends." He moved his fingers lower, parting her swollen folds and thrusting into the hot clench of her pussy. She tried to hold back her response, but a small whimper bubbled up from her throat.

"I'm going to cram this hungry little cunt full of my cock and do my best to draw those sexy noises from you while they speculate what we're doing and try to catch us fucking."

She shuddered as he made slow thrusts, tormenting her hot spot with each stroke and pinching her nipple at the same time. "Knowing they're so close and trying to be quiet is going to make your come flow over my cock and trickle down my balls, your heat mixing with the cool water. You're going to squirm and buck, beg me to move faster, but I'm in the mood to take my time. I'm going to go so deep with each long thrust, driving you mad with the need to come."

Kate began riding his hand. "Yes. Now, Jesse."

Damn it, he wasn't prepared. "Shit, I don't have a condom, honey. I was tested a few months ago and I'm clean."

"I'm on the pill, and my last test was normal. We can both go get retested again later. Please, don't make me wait. Fuck me."

He chuckled, pulled his fingers out of her intense heat and held the thin strip covering her slit to the side. A quick tug at his waistband and his cock was free. Kate wrapped her legs around his hips and the blunt head nudged against her entrance. She dug her feet into his ass, trying to pull him inside, but Jesse gritted his teeth and maintained a slow pace. He wanted her to feel each and every inch.

Her head fell back against the edge of the pool, eyes closed, an intriguing purring sound rumbling up from the back of her throat. Each noise was amplified by the water and walls of the pool to echo around them. The gentle slap of water against their skin kept time with each movement, drawing them farther into each other.

"Want another beer?"

The question came out of nowhere. At the sound of her friend's voice, Kate's head snapped up and her pussy squeezed his cock in a tight clench. She gasped, her eyes springing open wide in shock.

"Better answer her, honey, so she'll keep moving," he teased while nibbling on her neck.

"I-um...n-no thanks. I'm good."

"Mmm...damn good, Katie." Jesse pressed another pulsing inch of hungry shaft into her body as Tink paused and stared down at them.

"How about you, Jesse? Want a beer?"

Kate squirmed and he drove another inch deeper as she clawed at his chest. He wasn't sure if she was trying to push him away or pull him closer, but he was appreciating every moment of her discomfort and the havoc it created with her conflicting desires.

"Hmm..." The pregnant pause that followed brought out Kate's fiery attitude and she pinched his chest. "No, but thanks."

Tink walked away, but kept casting suspicious glances over her shoulder.

"You jerk!"

"Come on, Katie. You're loving every minute. I can feel how wet you are, and your burning hot cunt is gripping my cock tighter than a vice. I can barely move. You enjoy knowing they're watching."

Her teeth sunk into her rosy bottom lip, driving him wild. Jesse vividly pictured those lips spread around his cock, cheeks hollowing out as she sucked him so good. Almost as good as the wet velvet grip of her pussy. He was willing to bet her gorgeous ass would be even hotter and tighter.

Someone splashed nearby, but Kate seemed lost to their surroundings and didn't notice. The way she gave herself over to passion completely was such a turn-on.

Her strong muscles contracted, legs pulling him deeper. "That's it, Katie. Fuck me back. Forget everyone and everything else. It's just you and me."

By the time he was completely enveloped balls-deep within Kate, she'd overcome her apprehension of fucking in public and seemed to bask in the pleasure. Her pussy pulsed around Jesse and his ability to hold back melted away. He started drilling into her, drowning in every strangled cry, capturing each in his mouth.

As Tink made her way back over to the pool, one of the guys swam to the edge, not far from their corner.

"Did you bring a beer for me, Tink?"

"I've got something for you, and it's not a beer," she teased.

"Oh, baby."

She set her drink down on the deck then slid into the water and the man's waiting embrace.

"The two of them over there groping in the dark is making me horny," Tink complained.

Jesse clearly heard the whispered words.

Mike chuckled. "I can help you out with that."

Jesse nibbled on Kate's ear then whispered so only she could hear him. "See, they're guessing at what we're doing. Wondering if we're fucking. Just like you're starting to wonder how far Tink and that guy will go. Will they fuck with us right here? What do you think?"

"I...can't." She struggled with each breathless word. "Don't...please. Need to come."

"I know, Katie. You need it so bad. I'm gonna give it to you. First, I want you to open those pretty eyes and watch your friend. Don't take your eyes off Tink and I'll give you what you want."

"Can't..."

Jesse stopped moving. He found it more difficult to hold still since his feet barely touched the bottom, but he managed.

Kate's eyes popped open. "Jesse. Don't stop!"

He grinned. Knowing she was learning who controlled her body was a rush. Oh, she'd question him again, fight his dominance, but not as hard. "I'm right here, honey. Now do what I told you to and you'll get your orgasm."

"Shit!" She muttered the curse, but did as told.

Her lips were quivering, teeth chattering. He knew she wasn't cold. Heat rolled off her body, bathing him in delicious warmth. She was reacting to the adrenaline rushing through her system. Feeling turned on by fucking in public, seduced by his words.

As soon as Kate turned her head and focused on Tink, Jesse began moving again. He was close to the edge himself, his cock painfully hard and pulsing. The friction created by the bathing suit against his shaft felt good now, but he'd pay for it with chafed skin later. Oh well. He wasn't about to stop. His sac had drawn up tight and ached to release his seed.

"Tell me what you see."

"I-um...it's too dark."

Jesse chuckled. "I know it's dark, but there's enough light to see what's going on over there. Tell me, Katie."

Her heart pounded in a rapid, erratic rhythm against her chest. As she strained to see, the walls of her pussy hugged him tighter and flooded with her slick juices. She was getting turned on by watching too.

"They're kissing, and pressed close together. Tink's hand is holding his head and...oh my God. She's pushing him toward her breast. I think that's her top lying on the edge of the pool."

Jesse kept his pace slow and easy. He relished hearing the tremor in Kate's voice as she described her friend's activities.

"Mike's mouth is moving along her neck and...oh shit!" Kate's fingers dug into Jesse's arms and her back arched, raking her hard nipples over his chest. "Shane is walking over there."

Her eyes widened, but she didn't look away or stop her running commentary. "Shane just went down the ladder and is swimming over to them. Mike turned, putting his back into the corner and Shane is now running his hands over Tink's back. She's reaching behind herself and pulling his face around for a kiss."

"Mmm...sounds like a yummy ménage."

Jesse didn't have much interest in what was going on across the pool. Sure it was hot, but he had his hands full of everything he needed. In fact, he was having the most difficult time keeping his thrusts slow and easy. The incredible friction was driving him insane.

He reached between their bodies. Taking one taut nipple between his fingers, he twirled and pinched the sensitive peak. Sliding his hand down her flat tummy, Jesse traced circles around her clit.

"Oh, yesss..." she moaned.

Kate closed her eyes and nibbled on his earlobe. When he applied firm, constant pressure to the sensitive nub she trembled. He was so damn close, they both were, but he held back. He wanted to see how this chance voyeuristic encounter would affect her. Wanted to know if it turned her on.

"Open your eyes and tell me more, honey."

Kate was reluctant, but finally complied with his wishes.

"One of Tink's hands is moving beneath the water. It looks like... Yes, she's stroking Mike's cock. I can't tell what the guys' hands are doing, but her head just rolled back onto Shane's shoulder."

They were able to hear every gasp and moan emanating from the other group. The wicked sounds, and the knowledge of what was happening, made his cock swell even larger. Jesse gripped Kate's hips tight, fighting to stave off his impending climax.

Kate moved her legs higher around his back, tilting her pelvis and ensuring he slammed into her clit with each stroke. "Unh," she moaned. After that she seemed to lose the ability to speak, even though she continued to watch the trio who now moved in a similar rhythm to their own.

Jesse gave up on taking things slow. He moved faster, gave in to the forceful pull of her legs and hammered into Kate. It wasn't an easy feat to accomplish in this position, but he gave it his all. Each hard drive sloshed water between their bodies. She had her teeth sunk into her lower lip again, but was unable to prevent small moans from escaping as her body tightened around his.

"That's it, honey. Now come for me. Let them see how beautiful your pleasure is." Jesse gritted his teeth, fighting to hold back his own release until she came.

When her orgasm hit, he wanted to shout in triumph as strong muscles sucked at his cock. A few more punishing thrusts and he climaxed, hot come spurting out to fill her greedy pussy. He branded her body, marked her as belonging to him. Filling her with his seed was another way of letting her know she was his.

She melted against him in the aftermath of their spent fervor, soft curves fitting against his hard planes perfectly. The gentle slap of water and breathy sounds coming from the other coupling made his cock twitch with interest, readying for Kate again.

He'd never felt this strongly before. The siren in his arms was the one. There was no doubt. She was everything he'd ever wanted in a woman. Bold and confident, a smart business woman, incredible artist, and beautifully submissive. Jesse was certain she felt it too, deep down in her heart. Now he just had to find a way to convince her to accept his love. If he had to wait, then he'd wait. She was worth the effort, the sacrifice, every moment of his time. It was that simple.

Chapter Eight

Kate's legs were wobbly and her hands trembled as she gathered up her belongings. A bright red flush covered her pale cheeks. Her bathing suit felt as if it was on upside down and inside out. She leaned over a lounge chair, let her hair fall over her face, and snuck a glance at Jesse from behind the sodden mass of tangled curls.

How the hell did he do it? Once again he'd fucked her into oblivion, and boy did it show in her disheveled appearance, yet the bastard showed barely any sign of their activities. His thick brown hair looked impeccable. Even standing there in his wet boxers nothing seemed out of place.

How annoying!

They hadn't talked about him going to her apartment. It was a foregone conclusion. Once she'd gathered everything, he came over and took most of the heavy burden from her arms.

For some unfathomable reason the show of manners pissed her off. She didn't want him to be nice in the aftermath of their mind-blowing sex. It made her uncomfortable, breaking down barriers and tugging at her heart.

How did he do this to her? Once again they'd had incredible sex, but instead of feeling happy and sated, Kate was pissed. Jesse had said they needed to talk. All they'd managed to do was fuck like bunnies. In public. With her friends and neighbors all around them.

Fuck!

She didn't care for dominant behavior in men. Not outside the bedroom. It made her feel stubborn, and gave her the need to prove...something. But Jesse was different. When she was with him, Kate wanted to follow every raspy command. One gruff order from his lips and she was putty in his hands.

When they reached the apartment, he took her key and opened the door.

"Just put everything down in the kitchen. I'll sort it out later." She had too much on her mind to worry about washing dishes. Kate left the door standing wide open on purpose as a not very subtle hint it was time for him to go.

After setting everything down, Jesse turned and headed toward the door, making her squirm under the heat in his eyes. She was relieved he was going to leave without an argument, but also experienced a bit of disappointment.

The sound of the door closing seemed so final. Kate let out a sigh of frustration. Her peeping cowboy had her all wound up in an emotional tangle and apparently no intention of giving her a moment to recover.

She turned with a gasp at the metallic snick of the lock sliding home. A sharp jolt of excitement tightened her chest and sent shivers of anticipation dancing over her skin.

"W-what are you doing?"

A devious gleam sparkled in his eyes as he moved across the room looking dark and dangerous. Determined and sexy as hell.

"We still haven't had our talk, Katie."

"Oh." Well, that sounded totally lame. And she had no idea why it didn't bother her anymore when he called her Katie. The nickname seemed different when he said it for some reason. Jesse's lips turned it into more of an endearment than an altering of her name.

"What would you like to talk about?" Duh! She wanted to recall the words as soon as they left her mouth. Seeing him stand in her living room wearing only a damp pair of boxers was doing funny things to her brain.

She watched him pick up the towel from the stack of things he'd carried up from the pool, then turn and walk toward the couch. Golden skin stretched taut over his sinewy torso. The wet shorts clung to his muscular ass closer than a second skin. She was mesmerized watching the firm cheeks clench with each movement. A spattering of dark hair covered his thick legs.

He was careful to spread the towel over the leather surface before getting comfortable. Kate appreciated his thoughtfulness.

"Come here, honey."

Her feet started moving without direct permission from her brain when he extended a hand. She couldn't pass up the inviting idea of snuggling into the comfort of his body.

She shrugged, not wanting to talk about herself. She'd had an average childhood and the past few years, a pretty boring life spent devoted to work. There wasn't much to talk about. She'd much rather hear about him. "You first."

They talked about anything and everything, sharing bits and pieces of their lives. Kate found herself relaxing into the easy conversation. She enjoyed listening to Jesse's stories about ranch life and his friends. His expression turned wistful and she detected an underlying longing in his voice while he spoke of happy times.

"Rainy days are boring. We wind up doing jobs which have been put off for some time. Repairing tack for the horses, and washing mounds of laundry. Those days are good though.

Everyone gets antsy because we know once the sun peeks through the clouds we'll be heading for the north pasture."

"And what happens in the pasture?"

Jesse chuckled. "That's where we play. Sometimes it's basketball on ATVs or even skiing down the muddy hill."

"Oh man. I'm picturing the Gretchen Wilson music video where she's zooming around on an ATV slinging mud everywhere."

"That's pretty close. By the time we're done playing, you can't tell who's who under all the dirt."

Kate shook her head. "Doesn't sound like any ranch I've ever heard of before."

He nodded toward her laptop sitting on the coffee table. "You got that hooked up to the internet?"

"Of course."

She grabbed the computer, got it started and handed it over. He typed in a web address and the intense longing was back in his expression. Jesse showed her pictures and talked about the Shooting Star ranch with obvious pride. She was shocked to discover what a huge undertaking it was to run the twenty thousand acre enterprise.

It was a beautiful spread of land. They browsed through images of unobstructed blue skies, open green pastures, and towering mountains. In the summertime the mountains were bronzed stone dappled with golden sunlight. In the winter, they wore a stark white blanket of snow.

He pulled up a picture of a huge lake. Golden grasses appeared to waver in the breeze along the shore line. Jesse pointed out a small boat house. "We have a speedboat, jet skis, canoes, and kayaks. There's even a course of ramps and obstacles for when we ski."

There were several images of a huge ranch house, corrals full of prancing horses, and a large stable. She found the property to be beautiful and rustic.

A bright smile teased the corners of his sensual mouth as Jesse came to a picture of a tall, curvy woman with long blonde hair standing next to a beautiful brown horse. "This is the ranch owner, Savannah Black, and her horse, Moon Dancer. Van breeds prize winning horses."

In the next picture, Savannah stood with her arms wrapped around the waist of a serious looking cowboy with stunning blue-gray eyes. "This is her husband, Cord. He's the ranch foreman. He's not real fond of the games Van dreams up, but lets us indulge in some wild fun as long as it's not dangerous. There was one time when Brock, one of the hands, could have been seriously hurt while jet skiing on the obstacle course."

Four handsome cowboys, including Jesse, stood with their arms slung over each other's broad shoulders in another picture. "This is Brock." Jesse pointed out a man sporting a sable mustache and a no nonsense expression. "He's the most levelheaded of the motley group. This is Zeke." A feeling of quiet innocence surrounded the sandy-haired cowboy. She wasn't sure if it was because of his cornflower blue eyes or his open expression. "He's the baby of the group and is a bit shy."

Jesse chuckled, skipped over himself and pointed to the man on the right. "This is our prankster, Riley." The man he indicated had bad boy full of mischief written all over him. Jet black hair hung down into his sapphire blue eyes. "He's always finding ways to scare the hell out of Tamara."

After a moment of searching, he pulled up an image of a petite woman with shoulder length mahogany hair and jaded green eyes. "Tam's had it rough, but is coming out of her shell with the help of Dakota." The man's Native American heritage was easy to see in his long blue-black locks, cinnamon-toned skin, and nearly black eyes. "He's the newest addition to the ranch family."

Jesse pointed to a small group standing before a quaint cabin. "This is Craig and Sandy Morton, along with their daughter Mandy." They all shared similar shiny brown hair. Craig's eyes were brown, while his wife and daughter shared reflective hazel eyes. "Van saved Mandy when she was abducted by a neighboring rancher."

The tale of Wyatt Bodine chasing down the girl and imprisoning her in a cavern brought tears to Kate's eyes. She was riveted as he spoke of Savannah's visions of the girl. The bold woman risked her life in a rescue attempt. Riley and Mandy became very close and the Morton's had been adopted into the close-knit ranch family. It was apparent how much Jesse cared for and missed his friends.

He gazed affectionately at a picture of a woman with wavy brown hair and blue-gray eyes. This is Stephanie Black, Cord's little sister." The resemblance was uncanny. "Riley and Steph are fighting a serious attraction," Jesse confided.

"You would love the ranch." His tone turned wistful. "I'd love to take you there. Take you for a sunset horseback ride, show you around the ranch."

"It looks beautiful." The words came out whisper soft as emotions clogged her throat. She wrapped her arms around the big cowboy, attempting to ease his yearning to be with his friends.

He leaned back and stared into her eyes for a long moment. "I've spent enough time droning on about the ranch. Tell me about your family. Where did you grow up? Do you have any brothers or sisters?"

Kate sighed. "There's really not a lot to tell. I'm an only

child born to older parents who'd been told they wouldn't have children. We had a quiet, happy life. They've both passed on. Now it's just me." Kate didn't want to talk about her parents. It made her feel lonely and depressed.

"I've always been into art and computers so it was natural to combine the two. One day I hope to start my own company." She grabbed his hand and pulled Jesse up from the couch. Talking about her work was exciting, and she found herself wanting to share it with him. Kate gave him a saucy smile. "Come on, cowboy. I'll show you my etchings."

As she'd hoped, the joke lightened the mood, which had become way too serious. This thing between them was happening so fast, but felt good.

He'd had no idea the framed artwork adorning the apartment walls had been created by Kate's hand. Not only did she produce amazing graphic masterpieces on the computer, but vivid drawings in a variety of media. Colorful watercolors, stunning charcoals, and edgy pen and ink sketches captured the eye and imagination.

"These are incredible, honey. Have you ever considered selling some of them or doing a gallery exhibit?"

Her cheeks filled with a pink blush. "No. Then it would become work. My drawings are for my own fulfillment and enjoyment. Putting them up for sale would change how my art makes me feel. Creating something solely because it makes me happy is much different than having to worry about what someone buying my work would want to see."

A series of charcoal landscape drawings made him think of the ranch and heightened his need to go home. "These are beautiful, Katie. They make me feel like I'm there, part of the scene at that moment." He turned and drew her into his arms.

"You have to come to the ranch. I'd love to show you around and see how Montana inspired your art."

Her eyes became distant and he glimpsed apprehension in her expression. She was right not to make any commitment to taking the trip with him. They'd known each other such a short time. He decided to let the idea go for now, but was not giving up on getting her to the Shooting Star lands.

Kate yawned and covered her mouth. He couldn't prevent his thoughts from turning to sex and once again thinking of how gorgeous her lips would look stretched around his cock. His blood rushed to engorge the randy organ, which stood up and tapped against his boxers as if saying, "Hey, buddy. Let me out to play."

Without giving her a chance to object, Jesse guided Kate into the bedroom and began tugging at her bikini strings.

"What do you fantasize about, Katie?" He untied the bow at her back and let the strings fall. "What makes you hot? Do you like playing with toys?" The top fell to the floor. Her nipples puckered and began to darken. "Do you want to be bound and pleasured until you're a quivering mass of raw nerve endings begging for release?"

Her breathing quickened, indicating the idea turned her on. His fingers trailed along her side, brushed the edge of swollen breasts, and came to rest at the curve of her hips. "What would you say if I wanted to share you with another man, one cock in your sweet pussy, the other in your tight ass?" Not that he'd share her, but a bit of creativity with a toy could provide dual penetration, if she desired it.

"Jesse..." she moaned as rich secretions penetrated the bathing suit and slicked her thighs.

"I'm right here, honey." He released the ties of her bottoms and let the material float to the floor. His fingers trailed over smooth skin to cup her rounded cheeks. "Have you ever been fucked in the ass, Katie?"

"No." Her breathy moan was almost unintelligible, but her desire was evident. She melted in his arms, body soft and ready for his possession. The sharp bite of her fingernails digging into his biceps increased his appetite.

Jesse pressed his knee between her legs to widen her stance. When his thigh came into contact with her wet heat it was his turn to groan. "What'll it be, honey? Tell me what you want."

Kate tipped her head back and stared at him from wide, green-ringed pupils. "I have some toys..."

His cock jerked, thumping against her belly. Toys were good. He liked toys.

"There's a box under the bed."

Since she didn't seem to be very steady on her feet, Jesse guided Kate to the bed. Once she was seated, he got down on his knees and retrieved a very large, rectangular box from beneath the bed. He glanced at her nervously chewing on her bottom lip, then opened the lid.

The container was divided into several different sections and contained enough paraphernalia to stock and adult toy store. He fell back onto his heels and perused the selection of butt plugs, nipple clamps, vibes, glass dildos, clit suckers, restraints, lotions and lubes.

"Holy shit, honey! I guess you really do like toys."

He picked up and discarded a few of the playthings. Kate's avid gaze followed every move he made.

"Tink has an online store. I test the products for her."

"You've tried out every one of these?" he asked in amazement.

Kate nodded.

"Which are your favorites?"

She pointed out a silver bullet and a vibrating egg sheathed in a bumpy purple sleeve. "I like those." Next she pointed to a long and slender black vibe in the butt plug section. "But that one's my favorite."

Jesse picked up the vibe, which bent in his hand. The flexible six-inch wand was attached to a controller by a wire. He set all three items on the bed and said, "Show me."

"W-what?"

"You heard me, Katie. I want to watch you. Play with your toys, honey."

Her eyes widened, but she nodded. "I'll need some lube and a towel." She squinted, scrutinizing her collection. "The dark purple bottle, please."

He grabbed the lube and fetched a towel from the bathroom. Instead of handing the items over, Jesse encouraged Kate to lie back on the bed.

"Lift up." He draped the towel over a pillow and arranged it so her hips were angled upward when she lowered back down.

A ripping sound filled the air as he yanked his boxers off then joined her on the bed. They shared a chaste kiss, but he refused to let it go very far or distract him. He parted Kate's slender thighs, creating a cozy spot to kneel in between, front and center. There was no way he was going to miss a second of the action.

"Show me," he repeated.

Kate reached out for the lube. He shook his head and popped the top. The pink folds of her pussy glistened with her arousal, but she'd need the added fluids to make using the anal probe enjoyable. With the towel in place, he didn't worry about making a mess and squirted a generous amount of the thick gel above her clit. He also dropped a large dollop onto her perineum. Jesse's attention stayed glued between her legs as the lube rolled along her folds and over the tight pucker of her anus.

His cock was painfully hard, and he absently stroked his engorged shaft. He didn't take his focus off his red fox as she plumped her breasts, tweaking the nipples with a firmer touch then he would've figured she'd use. She trailed one hand down to her navel, circling the indentation before dropping lower. Kate flicked her clit with a fingernail and moaned low in her throat. His heart pounded erratically against his rib cage. Damn, this show was liable to kill him, but he wouldn't miss it for the world.

"So hot, Red," he praised.

Snatching up the egg, Kate turned it on and teased her pussy lips with the tiny vibe. Once it was covered in a combination of her copious juices and the lube, she pushed it into her hungry hole. If her panting was any indication, the device snuggled up nice and cozy in the perfect spot.

"The probe..." she gasped. "Lube it up for me, Jesse."

Oh, fuck yeah. This was going to be blistering hot. Hell, it already was. His skin tightened in anticipation of watching her fuck her ass. Lying back on the bed, immersed in pleasure, she was the most beautiful woman he'd ever seen. Dark auburn curls fanned out over the ivory pillow case. Her pearly skin had turned pink, contrasting her nipples which were red as ripe berries. A light sheen of perspiration coated every succulent inch of flesh.

"Jesse!"

"Sorry, honey." He'd been lost in the sight of her, totally forgetting the toy. He grabbed the probe and slathered it with lube then placed it in her hand.

Kate wasted no time. She turned on the slender vibrator, rimmed her anus twice, then drove it into her ass with one slow and easy thrust, hips bucking up to take it deep. He stroked his cock, matching her driving pace.

"Yessss..." she hissed. Her hand grappled around the linens in search of the bullet. For such a tiny vibe it buzzed loud enough Jesse heard it over the thundering rush of blood in his ears. She played the bullet over her clit while thrusting the probe in her ass.

Jesse was on overload. The lips of her pussy were swollen and her narrow hole quivered around the black vibe. The air was leaded with the musky scent of sex and Kate's lusty moans. She worked her body hard, fucking her ass with an almost violent need, but her movements soon became uncoordinated and she lost the edge.

"Help me."

"Fuck!" Letting go of his cock, Jesse held both apparatus as she rode them. Damn if it wasn't the most erotic thing he'd ever witnessed. More so than anything in his wild past or group activities he participated in at the ranch. While he wanted to savor the sight longer, the desire was outweighed by his burning need to observe as the building orgasm sent her soaring.

"Now, Katie. Come for me now."

Chapter Nine

"Stop..." she gasped. "Too much!"

"No. Ride it out." Jesse's dominant tone and words both excited and irritated her.

Kate's body was coiled tighter than a spring ready to burst. She'd never been able to keep the stimulation going long enough to reach climax this way. With Jesse's help she was on the verge of something spectacular and frightening. The culmination of all those frustrating attempts.

While she wanted to reach out and seize the orgasm hovering just out of reach, she also battled the need to push his hands away. She was terrified of being swept away on the rising tide once the flood gates opened and changed her in some elemental way. What she felt was too powerful and mind-bending.

"Let go, honey. Fly for me."

Jesse was relentless in the pursuit of catapulting her over the crest. He played her body, drawing her in the same way the moon exerts its gravitational forces on the ocean, pulling her this way and that, bending her to his will. She was petrified of not being the same again.

He dialed up the vibrations on the anal probe and Kate was lost, no longer able to prevent the tide from engulfing her. She took a big breath to scream, but it became trapped in her constricted throat. All that escaped were choked, gurgling noises as every muscle in her body tensed. What happened next was akin to a thermonuclear meltdown.

Kate was familiar with clitoral and vaginal climaxes—the tightening followed by blissful tremors of release. This was different. The orgasm consumed her entire body, nerves firing off explosive pulses from the top of her head all the way to the tips of her toes. Her pussy spasmed around the egg, her clit fluttered wildly against the bullet, and her ass seemed to implode, sucking the probe deeper. Bright light burst behind her eyelids.

She wasn't sure but thought she might have left her body for a few seconds. A decadent feeling of weightlessness allowed her to rest until stunning aftershocks swept her up once again.

"Gawd damn! Fucking beautiful, honey."

She tried to respond but the words came out garbled as small tremors continued to surge through her. The only thing on her mind was curling up in a ball and riding the wave. When she finally came down, Kate was pleasantly exhausted and sated.

Apparently, Jesse had other ideas. He gently removed the probe from her ass, the slight friction reawakening the sensitive nerves. Katie groaned as he leaned across her hip. She heard the thunk of the toys being dropped into the box lid. The egg still hummed in her pussy, but she ignored it, too exhausted to remove the toy.

"My turn."

His turn? What one earth was he talking about? She'd had all she could handle in one night, thank you very much.

"Tired."

"'S okay. Need you...bad. Relax. I'll do everything."

Kate barely heard his voice from where Jesse hung over the end of the bed. When he knelt between her legs again, he held something in one hand and stroked his reddened cock with the other.

"Gonna need some lube."

She whimpered when the wide crown caressed her folds. Before she had the chance to offer a warning, Jesse eased into her pussy. He yelped and pulled out fast, rubbing his offended organ.

It wasn't funny. Not in the least, but she was unable to hold back her laughter. It bubbled up from her chest and passed her lips sounding a bit maniacal.

"What the fuck?"

Kate held her abdomen and shook. The combined expression of shock and insult on his handsome face was priceless. Once she calmed down, she dipped two fingers into her pussy and pulled out the buzzing egg.

Poor cowboy. He stared at the small toy pulsating on her palm as if it were some heinous torture device and gave her an evil-eyed glare for laughing over the incident. Too bad there wasn't a video camera running. The tape would win the top prize on Funniest X-rated Home Videos.

"Are you okay?"

His concern seemed genuine. For some strange reason it made her laugh harder.

"You won't be laughing anymore when I fuck your tight ass, honey."

The statement sucked all the humor from the situation and hot juices gushed in preparation. Her body agreed with the plan, but her mind harbored a few reservations.

"Nuh-uh." She pointed at his cock. "That's too big."

There was only one word to describe the grin which spread across his sensual lips—devious.

"You can take me. Gonna make it so good for you, Katie."

His burning stare melted her objections. She wanted this. Had yearned for the chance to explore anal sex with a suitable partner. Someone she trusted. A man capable of meeting her sexual needs. She hadn't known him for long, but Kate already trusted Jesse.

She nodded and began to roll over until he pinned her hips to the mattress.

"No. Stay put. I wanna be able to see your face, look into those pretty green eyes while I fill your ass."

Jesse would lose the last threads of his control if he didn't get inside her soon, but it was crucial to make this first time a good experience for Kate. He wanted her to crave having her ass fucked as much as he yearned to fuck it. Her emotions were written all over her expressive face. She wanted it, but had a healthy fear of the unknown.

"Gonna go nice and slow, honey. I want you to talk to me. Tell me what you feel. There will be some pain. That anal probe is nowhere near as big as my cock so first I'm going to stretch you with my fingers, get you good and ready."

His first lubed finger glided into her ass without any difficulty. When he added a second, the fit was tight. By the time he'd added a third, she was writhing on the mattress, riding his hand. Each panted breath made her tits jiggle provocatively, antagonizing him to lean forward and capture a taut nipple in his mouth. He sucked hard, greedy for the taste of her skin and sound of her gusty moans. Each nipple was given equal recognition until she was begging for more.

"Jesse. I want...please."

"What, honey. Tell me what you need and it's yours." He wanted to hear the words on her lips.

"Fuck me. Fuck my ass."

Before she finished speaking his fingers were out of the way and the head of his cock lined up with the fluttering hole. He sank past the snug ring of muscle, gritting his teeth in the struggle to hold back and give her time to adjust.

The lusty minx was impatient. She planted her heels into the bed and propelled her hips upward, engulfing half his length in the hot clasp of her ass.

"Give me all of it," she demanded.

The fierce need in her glassy gaze and harsh tone shoved past his self-imposed constraints. His inner beast broke free from its chains. Jesse grabbed her hips, fingers biting into soft flesh as he slammed forward until his balls slapped against her ass. His body moved in a frenzied pace, pounding her into the mattress. Kate gave back more than she took, meeting each thrust and delivering infinite pleasure.

"Fuck!" She yelled the word each time they crashed together.

Fat drops of sweat rolled off his face. His balls tightened, ready to burst. He wanted her to orgasm first, but not even the tight clench of her muscles strangling his cock could stop the come from erupting. He shouted her name as Kate found her own release and the narrow channel spasmed. The convulsions of her flesh dragged out his climax, drawing every ounce of seed along with his energy. He collapsed in a heap, flattening her spent body into the mattress.

"Ove. Evy." The gasped words were accompanied by a weak shove. With tremendous effort, his fried brain interpreted her meaning. He was crushing her. Jesse tapped into his miniscule reserve energy and rolled to his back. The new position at least allowed his deprived lungs to obtain much needed oxygen.

He was paralyzed, unable to lift a finger or move a muscle.

"Holy shit. You killed me," he complained. "I may not be able to move again."

The witch had the nerve to laugh about his predicament. Well, he'd teach her a lesson. Hell, he still owed her a punishment for ignoring their date, but disciplinary action would have to wait for him to recover if it was going to happen.

∞

A sudden flash of bright light had Kate pulling the covers over her head. She burrowed into the warm spot Jesse had recently vacated. Taking a large whiff of his lingering scent, she groaned as her sore pussy swelled. Damn, she was in big trouble if all it took was a trace of his essence to awaken her libido.

Incessant, happy humming assaulted her ears. Shudders of revulsion coursed through weary muscles. This was worse than she'd thought. The damn cowboy was one of them—a dreaded morning person. God could be very cruel at times. How had she missed this appalling trait over the past week he'd practically lived with her?

In the midst of her agony the most wonderful aroma teased at her nose. Ah, the precious, albeit addictive elixir with the power to breathe life into the near dead. Delicious nectar of the gods delivered to the civilized world by a Columbian saint and his donkey.

The bed dipped and she rolled, crashing against a solid lump. "Coffee," she croaked. The way-too-chipper heathen had the nerve to chuckle as she fought the blanket. Kate poked her nose out of a small gap, inhaling the rich bouquet of the hot beverage.

"You don't get the coffee until you come out of there."

Sadistic bastard. How entirely rude and extremely cruel to deprive the junkie of her morning fix.

She reached out with one hand, groping for the mug she knew lingered somewhere nearby.

"Ah, ah, ah. You have to pay first."

Pay? "How much? Name your price. My checkbook is on my desk. Write it out and I'll sign."

His hearty laughter annoyed her to no end.

"Money won't get you what you want, honey."

She groaned. "What will it take?"

"A good morning kiss will suffice."

Someone shoot me, please! A kiss. Her mouth felt pasty and her teeth wore fuzzy sweaters. Not even for coffee would she kiss him before brushing away the morning breath.

"Come on, sleepyhead. We have reservations at a local stable in an hour. Gotta get moving if you're going to have breakfast first."

"Reservations? For what? I have work to do."

The linens were unceremoniously yanked from her feeble grasp. Kate cringed, throwing an arm across her eyes. She didn't complain, secretly enjoying his playful nature.

"Today is Saturday, not a workday, and we're going riding."

Peeking out from under her arm, Kate took in the depraved maniac's evil grin. Dragged from her comfortable bed, Kate was forced into a lukewarm shower. Then the pushy jerk coerced her into eating a man-sized breakfast when all she normally had was a cup of yogurt and a banana.

The torture did not end there. She began to wonder if he'd stayed awake at night devising wicked ways to drive her insane. She did need the break from work though and gave in without much fuss. He drove to the outskirts of town where a bowlegged man presented her with a large horse. She reached out to pet its velvety nose and the mongrel blew a stream of gooey snot into her palm.

Über gross!

"Come on. I'll help you climb up."

Climb up? On the enormous beastie? Oh, hell no.

"I don't think so, cowboy. It doesn't look tame. In fact, it just gave me the evil eye."

Jesse threw back his head and laughed. *Jerk.*

Somehow he managed to sweet talk and hoist her into the saddle. Kate yelped as the horse snorted, then shifted its weight beneath her. Her gaze narrowed on Jesse as he effortlessly swung up onto his horse.

Damn if he didn't look good, too. She was finally awake enough to appreciate the sight of snug chaps covering his jeans and framing that grade-A ass. His big feet were encased in boots, and a pearl-buttoned shirt hugged broad shoulders. The look was topped off with the Stetson sitting atop his head.

The air rushed from her lungs in one gust. He truly was a real cowboy. She'd known he worked on a ranch, but seeing Jesse in his element was different, driving the idea home. He looked more relaxed and comfortable than she'd ever seen him, holding the reins gathered in competent hands.

The man was sex incarnate.

Under his expert tutelage, she soon had the knack of riding the animal, which turned out to be rather good-natured. They stopped by a stream to take a break and she fed the horse grass, laughing as its soft lips tickled her hand. When they returned to the stables, she was almost sad for the lighthearted romp to end.

Well, right up to the moment she dropped from the saddle and tried to stand. Kate would have fallen if Jesse hadn't arrived at her side in time. Her wobbly legs refused to support her weight and she now understood why the stable workers' legs bowed outward. It was not only painful when she attempted to walk, it was embarrassing as hell. She would have laughed if it didn't hurt so much. To make matters worse, she smelled of sweaty animal. Gross.

Kate gave Jesse the evil eye. If the bastard laughed she'd slit his throat.

"Say one word and you die," she warned.

Jesse fought the temptation to let go with a full belly laugh. She was adorable when irritated. Her hair was a windblown mess, and her light skin carried a pink tint from the sun. And her walk. Kate was walking stiff-legged, almost as if she had a broom stick up her ass.

She was perfect. For him.

Now he only had to convince her.

The past few hours of carefree fun, along with the casual conversations they'd had while learning about each other, should at least have his foot in the door. Add in the TLC he planned to lavish her with and the odds of getting Kate to open up more skyrocketed.

He'd been curious about her friendship with Tink, and brought up the subject during the return drive. "Tell me about your friend. How'd she get stuck with a name like Tink? Did her parents hate her?"

Kate coughed, sputtered, and spewed the water she'd been drinking over the dashboard.

"Shit, Jesse." She wiped the tears from her eyes after her choking episode subsided. "You almost killed me."

"Sorry, honey. I didn't know the question would send you into a fit."

She glared at him for a full minute, not answering the question until he asked it a second time.

"Tink's parents didn't hate her. Not when she was younger, anyway. Her family is rich, pretentious and stuffy—everything she isn't. They eventually disowned each other."

"Okay, but what about the name?" He'd been curious since first hearing it.

Kate pulled her lower lip between her teeth, torturing the soft curve. She appeared to be on the verge of telling him, but then closed up tighter than a clam.

"Tink is hypersensitive about her name. She'd be pissed if I told you."

Interesting. He let the subject drop, but made a mental note to find out the truth. How bad could her name be? "How long have you been friends?"

"We met our freshmen year in high school. Rode the same bus, which gave us lots of free time to talk."

"Wait a minute," he interrupted. "Why was the rich chick riding the bus?"

"Tink had moved in with her grandmother, who lived in my neighborhood. We became good friends. I had her back whenever she got into trouble, and she had mine when the 'in crowd' was cruel. Been together ever since."

He did a quick calculation. "So about twelve years?"

She eyed him warily. "Why all the sudden interest in Tink?"

From her telling reaction, Kate still ran interference for her friend. It was nice to know they were tight, but also meant convincing her to move away would be difficult. Each day he spent with Kate made him even more convinced they belonged together.

"Easy there, tiger. Just makin' conversation and getting to know you better."

Jesse pulled into his reserved parking space and turned to face her. "How about..."

She held up a hand. "I need a shower, some space, and a little down time."

They'd been together a lot. Taking a break was a good idea, but he didn't want to let her pull back too far. "Okay. How about we get together later for Chinese takeout and a movie at my place?" He glanced at his watch. "Around seven work for you?"

He held his breath until she agreed. The four hours were going to creep by. Hell, no sooner had she headed off toward her apartment then he was anticipating seeing her again.

ℂ

With a deep sigh, Kate lifted her hand and knocked at the door. Instead of attacking her mountainous workload, she'd spent the last few hours primping...

For a man...ugh!

This was bad. She didn't fuss over her appearance for anyone. Not even her ex-fiancé. People could either accept her or take a hike. Jesse was different, though. He made her feel different. She wanted to look her best for him. How ridiculous.

She'd taken a hot bath, shaved and rubbed lotion all over her body. She'd even put mousse in her hair and fought the rowdy locks into submission with a brush and blow dryer, forcing her curls to straighten. But what shocked her most was the length of time she'd spent dressing.

And she hadn't stopped thinking about him. They'd only been apart for a few hours, yet it seemed much longer. He had quickly insinuated himself in her life and become someone she depended on seeing every day.

This wasn't a date. They weren't even going out. What the hell was wrong with her? Looking down, she decided her outfit was outrageous. White daisy dukes, a form-fitting, low-cut red top and wedged sandals. It screamed "fuck me". She started to turn, prepared to go home and change.

All her concerns flew the coop when Jesse opened the door. Now there was one fine hunk of man.

Yup, she was doomed.

His eyes lightened to a pleasant shade of amber. Sensual lips curled upward and deep dimples bracketed each end as his gaze swept her from head to toe and back again.

Fresh from the shower, Jesse had on a black T-shirt and faded jeans. She felt envious of the soft clothing and its intimate contact with his sculpted muscles. His feet were bare, and his damp hair disheveled. Her thighs trembled as her pussy heated, panties growing damp in anticipation of riding the shaft lengthening behind his zipper.

He pulled the door open wide and motion off to the left caught her attention. Standing in the living room watching them was a handsome cowboy she recognized from his picture. The wavy sable hair softened his serious expression. Squint lines bracketed intelligent green eyes. The trim mustache over a soft pair of lips made her arousal flow as she wondered how the contrasting textures would feel brushing over her bare skin.

She cast a questioning glance at Jesse, wondering why the other cowboy was in Denver. Kate prayed he wasn't there to take Jesse home. A brief flash of pain tightened her chest as she stepped forward and thrust her hand out.

"Hello, Brock. I've heard a lot about you and the ranch. Nice to meet you. I'm Kate Brooks."

He was built similar to Jesse, tall and broad shouldered, maybe a tad wider across the chest. Thick, hard-earned muscles rippled as he reached out, his large hand swallowing hers. Graphic images of her slender curves pressed between the two solid men made her heart beat faster, her breath coming out in rapid pants which made her breasts jiggle, nipples tightening.

Brock's eyes filled with desire, his gaze lowering to her chest for a moment. A wicked grin flirted with the edges of his mouth and his nostrils flared, taking in the scent of arousal swelling between them.

"The pleasure is all mine, darlin'."

Jesse's menacing growl made her cringe. The randy cowboy held onto her hand, thumb stroking over the pulse fluttering wildly in her wrist, and laughed over his friend's jealous reaction.

Chapter Ten

The way Brock looked at Kate was about to put him over the edge. There was no way he'd share her. He would have to set Brock straight at the first opportunity.

Jesse had been surprised to find his friend at the door, grumbling about how miserable things were at the ranch. It appeared all the happy couples in residence were getting to him. Brock complained of finding them in the oddest places, kissing and groping. All Jesse could do was laugh. The situation was ironic. While he'd give his right nut to be at the ranch, Brock was running from home.

For the moment, he was stuck dealing with the randy cowboy.

"Why don't you two pick out a pay-per-view movie and I'll order dinner," Jesse suggested. He moved into the kitchen, but was still able to hear them arguing the merits of the available selections. They already sounded as comfortable with each other as old friends.

While they waited for dinner to arrive, Brock caught him up on the craziness at the ranch.

"Yesterday, I was minding my own business, walking past Tamara's cabin. I heard weird noises in the bushes and went to investigate. Dakota and Tamara were rolling around half-naked in broad daylight. Outside."

Brock shook his head and Jesse struggled not to laugh.

"Then this morning, I went into the main house to do some laundry. The washer in the bunkhouse is on the fritz again. Walked into the laundry room and Cord was fucking Van on top of the machine, which was in the spin cycle."

Hiding his smile behind his hand, Jesse made the mistake of glancing at Kate. She made no attempt to hide her mirth. Before he knew it, they were both laughing hysterically. Every time they looked at each other it made things worse.

"It's not funny when you aren't getting any," Brock complained. He shot an appraising glance at Kate.

Jesse pulled her closer. "Don't even think about it."

"What about the other guy?" Kate questioned. "The one who pulls all the pranks."

"Riley is too busy pretending not to notice Steph for anything else to affect him. We all know how Cord will react if he catches Riley sniffing around his baby sister."

Jesse grimaced. He'd witnessed Cord's wrath first hand. The man had a hot temper and overprotective nature when it came to the Shooting Star women.

The three of them laughed and joked through dinner, then turned on the movie. Brock settled in the recliner. Jesse sat at an angle in the corner of the couch and pulled Kate in between his legs. She wiggled around to get comfortable before resting against his chest.

The movie was a thriller. A steamy sexual journey through the addictive power of illicit passion, wrapped around a deadly mystery. As things got hotter between the characters on the screen, Jesse's cock took notice. Trying to be discrete, he released the button at his waist to relieve some of the pressure and rearranged himself.

Kate pressed back into him and shifted until the hard length rested between the round cheeks of her ass. The brat kept moving around, making his erection grow.

"Don't try me, honey." He whispered the words so only she would hear. Her response was to increase her movements. Jesse took it to be permission to play.

He glanced over at Brock. The other man appeared to be involved in the movie. Good.

The action on the screen intensified. The heroine teased the hero past the point of control. She danced in the rain, puckered nipples showing through her now transparent white top, and caressed her lithe body.

Jesse slid his fingers under the edge of Kate's shirt and let them rest on her flat tummy. He kept watching the movie as the heroine led her man upstairs, stopping frequently to indulge in very sensual foreplay.

His skin burned, cock twitching as the hero slammed his woman into the door for a hard screw. The man's hands cupped her ass, raising her and sinking deep inside.

Fuck! It was driving him crazy. Jesse let his fingers move upward, teasing Kate's peaked nipples through her lacy bra. He needed to touch bare skin. Deft fingers popped the front clasp, freeing the lush mounds. She squirmed as his fingers tweaked her sensitive nipples.

"Don't make any noise," he whispered, "unless you want Brock to watch. He'd join in if I let him, but don't count on it, honey. I'm not sharing you with anyone."

Jesse inched her shirt higher and higher, exposing her quivering belly. His fingers didn't stop teasing her breasts, which swelled under his manipulation. She hissed as the material rasped over her nipples seconds before cool air kissed her hot flesh.

Kate's gaze immediately shot over to where Brock sat. If the hard length pressing against his jeans was any indication, she was out of luck. Her gaze snapped up to his face. Sure enough, the cowboy's intent eyes devoured her bared breasts.

Not sure how to react, she decided to go with the flow and see where things went. Jesse licked the shell of her ear and nibbled on the lobe. The jerk knew she was susceptible to his dirty talk. He kept a running commentary going in a raspy tone.

"Look at Brock, honey. See how much your beautiful body turns him on."

Her gaze locked on the other man, watching his fingers brush his denim-clad erection. She couldn't look away from the seductive sight.

Jesse pulled the shirt over her head, tossed it to the side then cupped her breasts. His fingers massaged the firm globes, tugging at her nipples. Electric sensations zinged through her body, coalescing at her clit.

"He can look all he wants, but I'll kill him if he tries to touch you."

The possessive words made her adrenaline spike. Hot juices gushed from her pussy. She wanted more.

On the TV, the couple frantically fucked against the door, their moans filling the air. The sound of a zipper opening drew her attention back to Brock, who now held his shaft, pumping in an easy rhythm. In the low, flickering light from the movie, Kate saw a wet drop of fluid on the ruddy head of his cock. His thumb breezed over the liquid, spreading it with the next stroke.

"You've got him all hard and needy, Katie."

One of Jesse's hands headed south, disappearing beneath her waistband. The shorts were too tight for him to reach his goal.

"Let me in," he ordered. Without thinking about it, she popped the button and dropped the zipper. He played in her curls before lowering to caress her slick folds.

Staring into Brock's eyes, she wondered what he was thinking. Did he think she was a slut to let Jesse finger her while he watched? Did he want to join in? The idea of two men sucking on her nipples and fondling her sex made her even hotter, but also nervous.

Sensing her anxiety, Brock whispered, "Are you okay with this, Kate?"

Was she? Kate wasn't sure what to think, but she wanted to see where it went. The whole thing was turning her on more than fucking in the pool with her friends close by had.

Unable to voice a reply, she nodded.

"If it gets to be too much, tell us and we'll stop. I hope you'll let us keep going. This is so fucking hot, Kate."

Yes, Brock was right. Having him watch Jesse pleasure her definitely cranked up the heat.

One blunt fingertip circled her clit. Kate couldn't help bucking her hips into Jesse's touch. It may be wrong, but she enjoyed having Brock watch. Her gaze remained riveted to the strong hand palming his hard cock. She'd always found men masturbating to be sexy as hell.

Jesse gathered her cream on his fingers then pulled free of her pants. She whimpered at the loss, turning her head to follow the path of his hand. He inhaled her scent, closed his eyes, and proceeded to suck each finger clean.

"You taste so good, honey. Sweet and tangy."

Brock groaned and cussed under his breath, increasing the pace of his hand job.

She sighed when Jesse's hand returned to her pussy. Once

again he gathered her arousal, but this time he used it to paint her lips.

"Taste yourself, Katie."

Her tongue shot out to lick her lips. She'd tasted herself before, but in this situation it was a different experience, enhancing the flavor.

Jesse began working her shorts down over her hips. She lifted for him to make it easier. Her panties slipped down her legs with the shorts. When they hit her ankles, she worked the clothing off with her feet.

"Gorgeous," Brock praised.

Hell if she was going to be the only one naked. "I want to see some skin, boys."

Brock was all too eager, quickly shucking his shirt, boots and pants then resuming his casual masturbation. Jesse seemed reluctant to let go of her, but soon ditched his clothes. Maneuvering was difficult on the couch, but before long his cock nestled in the crevice of her ass. He was hard as steel, and although she was enjoying their erotic game, she wanted him inside her.

Kate squeezed her muscles, massaging his erection. Her hands roamed Jesse's sinewy thighs, nails digging into his legs as his fingers returned to tease her slick lips.

The weight of Brock's stare drew her attention back to the handsome cowboy who still wore his Stetson. She would have laughed, but Jesse chose that moment to thrust two fingers into her pussy.

"Unh," she moaned. Her head fell back on his shoulder as she rode his hand. Kate became lost in sensation, almost forgetting about Brock until he groaned. She glanced over to see his gaze riveted between her thighs. He pumped his cock in the same tempo Jesse drilled his fingers into her.

"Jesse. I need you."

His hands grasped her hips, lifted her above his lap then lowered her over his cock. Kate gasped as the thick head powered its way into her wet pussy. Without giving her any time to adjust, he set a rapid pace.

It was fucking amazing, the friction totally mind-bending, but she needed more.

"Fuck me harder. Faster." She bent her knees, digging her heels into the couch. With her hands braced on his thighs, Kate met Jesse's thrusts.

"Have mercy."

The words were muttered in a gravely tone from somewhere in the vicinity of her side. Her eyes snapped open, head swinging around to take in the show. Brock had moved closer, his cock only inches from her shoulder. She licked her lips, watching pearly liquid seep from the slit as he pumped the rigid flesh.

"Come for me, Katie."

"Can't."

"Damn it, honey. I'm going to explode. Come for me."

"I can't," she whined.

Brock studied Jesse's pained expression. "Let me help her."

"Fuck," Jesse mumbled. His expression turned fierce. "Touch her clit, but nothing else."

Oh, holy shit. The two of them acted like the decision was theirs to make, as if she had no control over anything. Her body tensed with irritation. She drew in a big breath, ready to give the two dominant jerks a verbal lashing, but ended up choking as a calloused finger circled the pulsing bundle of nerves.

Kate stared into Brock's glassy, dilated eyes. They were nearly black, the green a thin ring around huge pupils. Her body shuddered, muscles tightened, pussy clamping down on Jesse. The breath exploded from her lungs, bathing the steel spike Brock still palmed. White ropes of semen shot from the tip, hitting her breasts in a hot splatter.

Someone was screaming. It took a moment for Kate to figure out the rapturous sound emanated from her throat. Jesse wasn't far behind them. The hot splash of his come hit her womb and she collapsed onto his chest, panting as though she'd run a marathon.

With a heavy thump, Brock fell back. He barely seemed to notice. His eyes were clamped tight, his breathing erratic, sweat coating his muscular body.

She was turning into quite the hussy. Each new experience Jesse introduced her to brought out a wanton woman Kate didn't know lurked within herself. If their sex got any more wicked, she might become addicted.

Chapter Eleven

Jesse had heard about sparks flying between people, but had not witnessed the phenomenon before. He and Brock were getting ready to go out. Kate had gone home to get dressed, and showed up at his apartment with Tink in tow.

Electricity filled the air when Tink and Brock were introduced. Jesse swore he saw streaks of lightning pass between their bodies. The two fell into an odd game of push and pull. It was the craziest damn thing he ever saw. Brock started out turning on the charm, but it only made Tink act bitchier.

"Howdy, little darlin'." Brock tipped his hat, and grinned.

Tink groaned. "Who let the Lone Ranger here escape the ranch?"

Brock didn't hesitate to trade insults with the blonde bombshell. "Damn, Kate. Your friend here seems to need a bitchectomy."

"Ha. Good one, Tex."

"Not all cowboys are from Texas, darlin'. I hail from the Big Sky state of Montana."

"Looks like a Texan, talks like a Texan…must be a Texan." Tink's gaze trailed the length of him. "You know, only two things come out of Texas. Queers and steers."

Brock narrowed his eyes, staring Tink down. "I'm not from

Texas." He gave her the same thorough once over in return. "'Course, someone named after a fairy probably knows all about queers."

Tink's fists settled on her hips and she moved in closer, standing toe to toe with the tall cowboy. "I'm not named after a fairy. And even if I was, it's none of your business, Tex."

With his shoulders back, spine rigid, Brock was an intimidating sight. Tink didn't back down. The woman was either brave or stupid, but she held her ground.

"Why don't you fly back to the forest and sprinkle some fairy dust on lost kids."

Tink puffed out her chest, leaning in closer to her adversary.

"Why don't you climb back on the ass you rode in on and head back to Dodge."

Kate stretched up on her toes. "Should we do something?" She'd gotten close to Brock over the past few days, but Jesse didn't want her getting in the middle of whatever was happening between their friends. He shook his head. "Uh-unh. Don't get between a rabid dog and its bone. The two of them will find a way to work it out."

"He's hard and her nipples are poking out. I'm not sure if they're going to kill or fuck each other."

Unable to suppress his laughter, Jesse chuckled over Kate's comment. Tink and Brock didn't seem to notice. They were focused on each other. "Either way it goes, it'll be worth the price of admission."

"I'm putting an end to this nonsense." Kate charged headfirst into the situation before he was able to stop her.

"You two can spend the evening verbally fucking. I'm going out."

She marched right between the two, shoving them out of her way, and headed for the door. Jesse felt his cock stiffen. Damn, he loved a woman with some spunk. He followed in her path, throwing over his shoulder, "You 'bout done?"

Brock cursed under his breath. "Don't leave me here with the viper. The bitch is poisonous."

Jesse barely heard Kate comment. "I can't wait to see how they act in public."

The childish behavior continued as they climbed into his truck. Tink and Brock fought over who was sitting where until Kate decided it for them by sliding into the front seat next to him, leaving only the back available.

Kate watched Tink drop her purse on the bar and head off with her cell phone in hand as soon as they entered the club.

"Tink's up to no good. I better go talk to her before she pulls some stupid stunt."

Jesse took her by the arm, steering her toward the dance floor. "Let them work it out, honey. Dance with me."

She was reluctant to leave Tink to her own devices. The woman was dangerous when riled, and something about Brock ruffled her feathers. Kate had suffered the brunt of the woman's schemes too often, but the appeal of dancing with Jesse was a pleasure she wouldn't miss.

He held her close as they moved together, instinct and the music guiding their bodies. She loved the way they fit together, his hard muscles complimenting her softer curves. After several upbeat songs, she needed a break.

"Come on, cowboy. Buy me a drink."

Brock stood at one end of the bar, but Tink was nowhere in sight. This made Kate edgy. There was no telling what she was doing and no doubt it wasn't anything good.

"Where's the hellion?" Jesse asked.

Kate elbowed him in the ribs. She studied Brock, noting the tension in his jaw. He was definitely on the defensive.

"Hell if I know."

Dancing had made her hot and thirsty. Kate downed half the bottle of water as soon as the bartender set it down. She turned to survey the crown and her stomach turned. Tink was headed their way, her arm linked with an all-too-familiar man.

Kate placed a hand on Brock's shoulder, but never took her eyes off her friend. "No matter what happens, please try to ignore her. Let it go for me."

"What are you talking about?" He turned to see what had captured her attention. His entire body went rigid when he spotted Tink, and he rocked forward onto the balls of his feet.

"Tink," she warned as her friend got closer. "Please...,"

Tink ignored her. Brock held her undivided attention.

"Hey, Tex. I found a friend of yours."

The same man who'd put on the submissive show at the office had now turned effeminate. With an exaggerated, high squeal, he latched onto Brock.

"Oooh!" The man clapped his hands. "There's my hunky Texas cowboy."

He held tight to Brock, stroking beefy biceps and rubbing against him like a cat in heat.

Jesse's body tensed. Kate knew he'd back Brock in a fight. And damn Tink was doubled over, laughing her fool ass off. A muscle in Brock's jaw ticked and he looked ready to commit murder.

"Get your hands off me before I pound you into the ground," he warned.

Tink's accomplice turned toward the rest of the group. "He

gets so bashful when we're out in public." He lowered his voice to a soft tone and placed a hand next to his lips as if sharing confidential information. "Poor dear hasn't come out of the closet yet."

Brock glared at Tink. "Get your friend outta here or I'm going to tell everyone in the bar why your nickname is Tink. You've got ten seconds."

Oh, Lord. Saying that was akin to waving a red flag in front of a bull. Kate bit her lip, wondering if he actually knew the secret of Tink's name.

Tink's focus swung her way. Her friend's hard gaze promised painful retribution. Kate shook her head. "Don't look at me. I've never told anyone."

"Seven, six," Brock counted down in a cold voice.

"There's no way you have the goods, cowboy."

"You really want to test that theory?" His expression was doubtful. "Three, two..."

A crowd gathered around them to observe the spectacle. The two of them squared off, neither backing down, and Kate wondered if it would be a showdown at the OK Corral or Armageddon.

"Alright, you asked for it, Prunella..."

Tink's already hard expression turned to stone.

"Lucretia..."

Her body began to vibrate with bottled up rage.

"St. Claire hyphen Fitzmoore."

Her face turned beat red, and Kate swore she saw steam coming out of Tink's ears.

"I can hear your lovers now. Oh yeah, Prune, baby. You get me so hot." Brock's taunt was the final straw which broke Tink's temper free.

"Oh my God!" No one was able to keep from laughing over that one. The entire crowd surrounding them burst out in hysterical fits.

Tink got up in his face. "Dead. Man. Walking."

This was not good. Tink had a real chip on her shoulder about the name given to her by a pretentious, snooty family she didn't get along with. In fact, she was the black sheep of the family. They'd disowned her long ago for shunning their aristocratic ideals. The nickname had come from her childhood envy of the devilish, fun-loving fairy, Tinkerbelle, she'd read about. Not that she ever owned up to the fact. Tink had related to the fictional character instead of her hoity-toity family. And who wouldn't take a nickname if their real name was Prunella.

Kate had to cover her mouth in order to hide a giggle.

The right hook Tink threw came out of nowhere, knocking the big cowboy backward. He staggered a step then stalked forward.

"You're damn lucky I don't hit women, although I might have to make an exception for you, Tinkerbelle."

If Kate hadn't seen it with her own eyes, she wouldn't have believed it. The two of them were turned on again. Tink's nipples were hard points protruding from her breasts and a line of sweat formed above her lip. Brock sported a big bulge in his pants. Go figure.

"Dick!" Tink practically spit the word at him.

"What did you call me?" His eyebrow arched high above one eye.

"Need me to define it for you, Tex." An evil grin lit up her face. "A dick hangs around with two nuts all the time and lives next door to a real asshole. Has a head he can't think with, an eye he can't see out of, and his best friend is a pussy. Every time he gets excited, he throws up. And worst of all, his owner beats him all the time."

Now Brock was the one with steam coming out of his ears as his temper reached its boiling point. Kate nudged Jesse. "Would you do something?"

"What am I supposed to do, get them a room?"

Kate grimaced. "So not helping here. Damn men!"

"Leave them alone, honey. They're both enjoying this and will work it out themselves." She was getting tired of hearing the same thing from him. He'd seen how wild and carefree Tink was, but didn't know her like Kate did. She knew her friend was making up for all the years of having her spirit dampened by her family, yet she harbored a secret longing to settle down with the right man. One who could see through the pretense to the caring woman inside.

Kate disregarded Jesse's comment and insinuated herself between the angry pair. She didn't want to see Tink's fragile emotions get hurt. "Um...hey. Let's get out of here. You can settle this at home...in private."

Tink kept her gaze glued to Brock as she answered. "Nobody's going anywhere until I find out who he's been talking to. Fess up or Matt doesn't leave your side."

The actor, who must be Matt, raised his hand in protest. "Love ya, Tink, but not happening. I've got a life, babe."

"It's simple, *Tink*," Brock interrupted. "You left your handbag on the bar next to where I was sitting."

Oh, that was wrong in too many ways to count.

"You have no right going into my purse." Tink glanced in Kate's direction.

"Sorry, but I have to back her up on this. The contents of a woman's purse are private. Definitely none of any man's business."

Tink harrumphed in agreement, tossed a drink in his face, and sauntered toward the door. She seemed too frustrated to continue the fight.

Brock picked up a few cocktail napkins and calmly wiped away the alcohol streaming down his face. The tension eased from his body since Tink had left the vicinity. The man had no clue. He should be even more worried with her out of sight.

"Don't think this is over. Not by a long shot. She won't forgive you or forget. If I know my girl at all, she's off determining ways to make you suffer." Kate patted him on the shoulder. "Better watch your back."

ஐ

Kate plopped down onto the couch with a heavy sigh.

"It's a good thing Brock's visit is over. He and Tink would have killed each other if he'd stayed any longer."

At first the love-to-hate-you situation between the two strong personalities had been funny. Jesse had gotten a few good laughs out of their antics over the past few days. It got old real quick, though. The more they carried on, the more it wore on him.

No one had suffered more than Kate. There were dark circles shadowing her eyes, lines creasing her forehead, and she was exhausted. She'd tried to referee and maintain some semblance of peace between their friends, but it had been an insurmountable task. The two were bound and determined to butt heads at every turn. The tension this created, added to her massive workload, had taken their toll.

Time for some TLC.

He stood behind the couch, gathered her hair and moved it

over a slender shoulder which carried the weight of the world. Kate was a strong, driven woman. While he admired her tenacity, Jesse wished she'd let him relieve some of her burdens. She hissed as his fingers pressed into tight knots of muscle and began working out the kinks.

He decided what she needed was to get away. The ranch was the perfect solution. Not only would she get to relax, do some drawing, but he'd get to spend some time on the land he loved. A win-win situation.

"Is Riesman closing the office on Monday?"

"Oh, damn. That feels so good." Her head tilted to the right, giving him better access to work the left side of her neck. "What would he close the office for?"

"It's a holiday, honey. Labor Day."

"Oh, yes. A little to the right." The small sounds coming from Kate mixed with her unique scent. His blood surged through his veins, pooling in his cock, which now tented the front of his sweat pants.

"Do you have to work Monday?" This time the question was mumbled because of his tightly clenched jaw.

"D.H. will expect me to put in some time, even if everyone else has the day off."

Riesman was such an ass. "What if I offered to take you away for a long weekend?" She rolled her neck to the other side as his fingers crossed her spine. "We could fly out of Denver Friday night, spend a quiet weekend somewhere, and be back Monday night." The ranch was rarely quiet, but it wasn't something easily explained. Better she discover ranch life firsthand.

"Mmm," she purred. "Sounds heavenly. Too bad I'm so busy right now."

Damn it. He admired her strong work ethic, but hated the way Kate overworked herself for a jerk who didn't appreciate the effort. He wasn't going to let this golden opportunity to introduce her to the ranch pass them by. One way or another, he'd make this work.

Kate dissolved beneath his fingers, muscles softening, smooth skin heating. The long column of flesh dotted with a smattering of freckles invited his exploration. Touch wasn't enough.

He dropped to his knees behind the couch, nuzzling her nape and filled his lungs with her electrifying aroma. "It's impossible to be near you without touching." He continued to knead one shoulder. "And tasting." Licking a path from one freckle to another, Jesse reveled in her satin texture and flavor on his tongue.

Letting go, he sat back on his heels. It took a few seconds for the sensual haze surrounding Kate to thin before her head snapped around.

"Jesse." His name was a breathless moan. A sultry plea for more he struggled against.

"Hmm?"

"D-don't stop."

Putty in his hands. He nibbled on her earlobe and rested his fingertips over her collarbones. "Say yes, honey."

"Huh?"

His fingers grazed her jaw, turned her face. There was no resisting the temptation her rosy lips presented. Jesse traced the lush curves, licked across the seam, and then inside when she opened for him. Kissing Kate made him think of summertime on the ranch—warm, fresh, ripe. She was the sun-kissed breeze in his hair, raspberries drenched in rich cream, the excitement of racing over the meadow.

She gasped in shock and shrunk into the cushions as he hurtled the sofa in one large leap. Landing next to her, Jesse grasped her hips and hoisted her into his lap.

"Say yes to a weekend trip."

How the hell did Jesse expect her to answer questions? She was hot and horny, the hard ridge of his cock compressed beneath her empty pussy.

"Need you!" Material ripped as she struggled with his shirt. The two of them became a rolling confusion of arms, legs, clothes and frenzied need. Her back hit the floor and the breath rushed from her lungs. Jesse's raspy chuckle was beautiful music to her ears.

Calloused fingers brushed along her ribs. She squealed and wriggled beneath his teasing hands in a desperate attempt to escape the torture. The cad followed her slithering body, ferreting out each sensitive spot, driving her into a convulsive fit.

How she managed to wriggle from his grasp was a mystery to be solved later. Kate raced for the safety of her bedroom. Two more steps and she'd be safe. She reached for the door...

Big arms wrapped around her middle. Jesse tackled her, twisting as they crashed to the floor to land cushioning her fall.

"Stop...please," she gasped.

"Say yes."

What the hell had the question been? Kate didn't remember or care. She would agree to anything if it brought an end to the devil tormenting every ticklish trigger point on her body.

"Yes. Okay. Just cut it out."

The beast growled, flipped them over, and buried his face between her breasts. Her oxygen deprived lungs sucked in huge draughts of air, her chest working overtime to meet the needs of her body.

This man was a danger to her heart. No other had made her laugh with wild abandon or initiated carefree play during sex before. He took her from blazing desire to sheer joy and back again, boggling her mind in the process.

I'm in love!

A bolt of lightning striking her chest would not have delivered a greater shock. She'd cared for Robert, but what she'd felt for her cheating ex came nowhere close to this new emotion making her heart beat faster. Their relationship hadn't been love. Affection wasn't even the right description.

How the hell had she gone and fallen in love with someone who would leave? It was only a matter of time. Jesse had made it clear his stay in Denver was temporary, limited to business. Once she finished the designs, he'd be history. *Hasta la vista.* Don't let the door hit you in the ass on the way out.

Fuck!

"You're thinking too much."

Am I over thinking it? Kate had no idea. This was strange new territory. Did he expect her to treat their time together as a casual affair? A pleasant memory to pull out when she was old and wrinkled.

"Kate, you're scaring me."

Scaring him. She was already past scared and bordering on petrified.

Yoga, think yoga. Breathe. Good air in, bad air out. Find my center. Oh, God. He'd pulled the ground right out from underneath her.

Distraction. She had to distract him. "I need you to fuck me now, Jesse."

Chapter Twelve

Why the hell did women have to make traveling so complicated? The last few days had been a whirlwind of activity. Thank goodness he'd had Tink's help, otherwise Jesse wouldn't have made it through the ordeal. Kate had thrown one obstacle after another in his path. The very idea of escaping from work for a few days of rest and relaxation put her into a tailspin.

You wouldn't know it looking at her now. She lay sleeping in the car while he drove. The peaceful expression on her face was a nice switch from the lines of strain which appeared when she was awake.

Work had been her excuse for not going until Tink interceded, showing up at the apartment going on and on about how D.H. wanted everyone to enjoy the holiday by taking time to recharge. It was a good thing the unflappable woman was on his side. If Tink got it into her mind to move the mountains, he had no doubt she'd find a means of manipulating the earth to do her biding. She was a veritable force of nature and a good friend to Kate.

Jesse and Kate flew out Friday night and stayed near the airport, saving the drive to the ranch for morning. He planned on making the most of the short stay.

He also hoped a few days at the ranch would help form a stronger, lasting connection between them. Something had happened the other night, and it was driving him nuts trying to figure it out. They'd been having a good time, laughing and playing, then all of a sudden Kate's demeanor had transformed. An odd tension jammed a wedge between them.

Still, they'd shared a special, almost immediate and undeniable connection. It was a good foundation. He'd found her guard dropped and she became the most willing to talk about herself when drowsy and sated after sex. In those intimate moments, she'd given him a glimpse of her beautiful soul.

His attention was divided between the road and Kate. She had crawled under his skin, become a part of his being, and he'd have it no other way.

Wiggling in the seat, Jesse repositioned the erection straining against the confinement of his jeans. Blood surged through his veins as his gaze moved over pink-painted toes and mile-long legs. She was curved in all the right places with perfectly proportioned breasts. Soft and feminine. Fiery. Red hair framed her face, making the freckles across her nose stand out.

The front tire dropped down into a pothole and the truck swerved. He overcompensated, and wound up with the left tires on the road, the right on the soft shoulder. By the time he got the vehicle under control perspiration had popped up on his forehead and over his lip.

He glanced over at Kate. All serenity was gone from her expression. One hand gripped the dashboard, the other clutched an armrest.

"Sorry, honey."

"What the hell happened?" She blinked rapidly.

"There was a deer," he lied. "Jumped right out in front of the truck."

One hand went to her chest as if attempting to keep her heart from escaping. She turned in the seat and stared out at the empty road behind them.

"I don't see any deer."

"Um...it ran back into the tree line." Reaching over, he soothingly rubbed her arm. "Did you sleep well?"

She flipped down the visor and stared into the mirror, fluffing her hair. "I had a weird dream."

He waited for her to elaborate, but instead, Kate changed the subject while touching up her lipstick. "How much longer until we get there?"

"It's not far now. We should reach the ranch drive in about twenty minutes. It's about five minutes from there to the main house."

"Hmm..." She flipped the visor closed. Turning sideways on the bench seat, she shot him a sultry glance, soulful eyes peering from under dark lashes. "However will I keep from becoming bored?" The last was purred, a suggestive grin curving her lips.

"I've...um, gotta watch the road for deer and other wildlife."

She unbuckled her seatbelt, scooting closer across the seat.

"That's not a good idea, Katie. Buckle up and stay on your side of the truck."

She tucked her legs up underneath her, rose up to her knees, and continued to move closer until she pressed against his side. Her fingers threaded through his hair, nails lightly scraping over his scalp and sending shivers skating down his spine.

Her tongue traced the shell of his ear. Teeth nibbled on his lobe. She blew a soft stream of air on the now damp skin and he jerked, causing the truck to swerve.

"I'm hungry."

The husky whisper had every muscle tightening, his cock sitting up and begging for attention.

"Honey, I'm trying to drive."

Her hand caressed his cheek, roamed over his neck, fingers slipping beneath his shirt collar. "And doing a damn fine job."

Pink fingernails raked his chest. "Keep your eyes on the road, baby."

With a deft flick of her fingers, she popped open first one button, then another. Each bit of skin revealed was sensitized by the scrape of her nails before being soothed by the warmth of her tongue. The lower she moved, the more fractured his concentration became.

How the hell was he supposed to drive while she poured over his body sweet as melted chocolate?

A twist of her wrist and the button on his jeans parted.

"Katie," he grumbled in warning.

His zipper gave way and the minx giggled as his cock spilled into her waiting palm. Forgetting all about what he was supposed to be doing, his gaze dropped to the slender hand circling his length. She seemed mesmerized by the pearly drop of fluid sliding over his crown. The tip of her tongue parted Kate's luscious lips and left a damp trail over the plump flesh.

Jesse had no trouble picturing her lips wrapped around his cock, painting his flesh with her lipstick as she sucked him to the back of her throat.

She stretched out on her belly, breasts flattened against his thigh, and licked a path from base to tip.

He'd never met a woman who enjoyed sucking cock more than Kate. Her tongue bathed his shaft, fingers massaging his balls, mumbled sounds of pleasure sending shock waves through every nerve ending.

The sharp drag of teeth along the ridge had his eyes snapping open. Damn! It was a miracle he hadn't run off the road yet.

Fuck this!

He slowed the truck and pulled off onto the grass, maneuvering them between some trees. There was no one else on the road, but he didn't want anyone pulling over to see if they needed some help. And hell if he was going to keep one eye on their surroundings. He planned on losing himself in the hot, damp suction of her talented mouth.

She glanced up, letting his cock slip free, and made eye contact as he thrust the gearshift into park.

"Don't stop now, Katie. You started this. You're going to finish it."

Damned if she wasn't turned on by his command. Kate ground her drenched pussy against the seat, but the slight friction wasn't enough. She needed more.

Sucking cock had always made her hot. Going down on Jesse turned her body into a raging inferno. His unique scent and taste released a voracious carnivore, made her insatiable. Her tongue traced her lips as the anticipation of sucking his engorged cock built. She devoured him with her gaze and her mouth salivated, her lips dying to stretch around his wide girth.

She was driven to put everything, heart and soul, into giving him pleasure. Her body hummed, awaiting the sublime thrill of his cock in her mouth. All the licking, sucking, nibbling. Tongue stroking and flicking. Lips gliding up and down while he pumped his hips to meet each movement.

Time to feast.

Her tongue skimmed over the silky crown. She loved how

every sense became involved, reveling in the soft texture of skin stretched tight over rock hard muscle. The frantic beat of his pulse pounding through enlarged veins. His weighty balls drawn tight and nestled in her palm. Sudden blasts of salty flavor inundating taste buds. The utterly masculine scent of his enjoyment.

She thrived under the challenge of pushing past her natural gag reflex, working to take more of his length, drawing in every inch she could manage. Relaxing her throat until she swallowed the head of his cock. Fighting past the initial panic of not being able to breathe.

It wasn't about having power over his pleasure as the act had been in the past. With Jesse her goal was to blow him away, give back as much of the incredible delight he gave as was possible. His satisfaction fueled her own.

His hands fisted in her hair, hips thrusting, fucking her mouth. She made loud slurping sounds and hummed against his cock in response to his guttural moans. He was getting close. So was she.

Pushing up onto her knees, she slipped one hand beneath the hem of her skirt and into her soaked panties. The swollen lips of her sex were slick with her hot juices. The rasp of a fingernail over her distended clit created a blinding combination of pleasure and pain. Driving two fingers into her empty cunt, she rode her hand.

"Oh, fuck. So good, Katie. Suck me harder."

Jesse's hips thrust faster, fucking her mouth with wild abandon. She hung on the precipice for what seemed forever, unable to push herself over the edge.

"Unh! Gonna come." He gasped, then his tone became firm, demanding. "Come with me. Now, Katie!"

His dominant control sent her flying. She drew in a large

breath and swallowed hard, finessing the final inch into her mouth. An agonized male howl that was also ecstasy filled the air as her throat constricted and drew against his cock. She devoured his tangy essence, her body convulsing, pussy clamping down on her fingers, and wave after delicious wave of rapture swamping her.

Sucking in large gulps of air, she collapsed onto his lap. The coarse hair covering his thigh tickled Kate's cheek. She kissed and nuzzled Jesse's now deflated shaft, wondering how she would manage to give him up when he moved back to the ranch. It was going to kill her inside, but there was no chance of a city girl holding onto a country boy.

Her career was tied to the city, and she had every intention of succeeding. Even if he stayed with her, Jesse would get tired of all the time she spent working. Hell, he already complained about it and she knew it would only get worse with time. She didn't want her commitment to her craft coming between them, but knew it would in time.

ℰↄ

A blind person would have seen the bond between Jesse and the tiny brunette who flew into his open arms, small breasts flattened against his chest as he held her close. It was in the tender way he greeted her and whispered words Kate wasn't able to discern. The underlying intimacy shared between Jesse and Tamara created a painful ache in Kate's lungs making it difficult to breathe.

He'd had sex with this woman.

A small crowd gathered around them. Jesse was patted on the back by the men, and hugged by a curvy blonde with great enthusiasm. The ranch owner's picture hadn't done her justice. Savannah was gorgeous. Even with the rounded belly and her child growing inside. She glowed with warmth and happiness.

Kate groaned. Were there any women on the ranch he hadn't fucked?

She shook hands and forced a smile onto her lips when introduced to his friends. The men were quick to drag Jesse off to see some new ranch equipment. Tamara confided this was code for new high-priced toys.

Kate was drawn into the house where she met the plump cook. She liked Millie on sight, knowing there was no way Jesse had slept with the older woman. At least there was one person she could relax around.

"Gonna have to fatten you up a bit. You're way too skinny," Millie complained.

Before she managed to form a protest, Kate found herself seated at the table behind a plate of cookies and an ice-cold glass of milk.

She was surrounded. Millie sat on one side of her, Tamara on the other, Savannah straight ahead. They began a brutal interrogation, making Kate feel as if she sat under a hot, bright light. Sweat broke out on her forehead as she fielded a barrage of questions.

"How did you and Jesse meet?"

"How long are you two staying?"

"Will you draw something for us?"

Her head snapped from one woman to another feeling as if she was in the middle of a tennis match. Thankfully, Steph walked into the room, saving Kate from answering. The woman's blue-gray eyes, an exact duplicate of Cord's, made her easily recognizable as his sister.

Introductions were once again made, and a bit of the tension eased from Kate. From the way Jesse had talked about Steph, she knew he hadn't slept with the friendly if somewhat shy woman.

Okay, so he'd fucked two out of the five women who lived on the ranch. And those two were both married now. The other woman she hadn't met yet was also married, and Millie was old enough to be his grandmother.

Tamara laughed so hard she doubled over. Steph gasped and Savannah grinned.

Fuck! She'd said that aloud. How freakin' embarrassing.

"Don't hold your punches," Tamara teased. "I like your style, Kate. You're going to keep that randy cowboy on his toes."

She could deal with this. Push past the mortification and consider the facts. She and Jesse both had pasts. Neither one had been virgins. Not even close. No point getting worked up about ancient history. Taking a deep breath, she struggled to remain calm.

The rapid fire questioning began again after barely a pause, the women talking over one another, giving her no chance to respond. It made her head swim.

"Let the poor child breathe," Millie chastised.

"Oh, like you weren't trying to get the 411 too," Tamara griped.

Kate couldn't help laughing. Tamara's spunk reminded her of Tink.

"Come on." Savannah stood and took Kate's hand. "I'll show you to your room so you can get settled in. You can meet Craig, Sandy and Mandy Morton later on."

She let the blonde lead her away. The conversation continued as they headed up the stairs.

"Van will discover all the juicy tidbits." Tamara's voice held obvious humor.

"Back off and give her a break before you scare her away." Steph's reply showed she was capable of holding her own and maybe wasn't quite as timid as she first appeared.

Kate was busy performing a quick calculation in her head. Four cowboys, an Indian, the ranch owner, her friend, Cord's sister, the cook, and the Morton family. An even dozen. This was one huge ranch family.

Actually, one of the cowboys was at school so there were only eleven names to memorize. Eleven people to make a good impression on. Great!

Why the hell had she agreed to this trip?

Savannah pointed out the location of the bathroom and guided her to a quaint room at the end of the hall. The window was covered by lace curtains. An inviting, four-poster bed was draped with an embroidered quilt. Crocheted pillows of different shapes and sizes crowed against the headboard.

The house was huge. All the furniture sturdy and heavy. The whole place reminded her of the old TV show, *Bonanza*. She half expected Little Joe, Hoss, and Adam to ride up on their horses and the Asian dude, Hop Sing, to run out of the house going off on a rant.

"Don't let them overwhelm you." Savannah drew her into a comforting embrace. "We're all excited to have you here, and to have you as a part of our family."

Part of their family? Talk about overwhelming. And how did Savannah know she was freaking out over facing so many of Jesse's friends? Either she was being very obvious or the ranch owner had some major intuition.

"I'm so happy Jesse found you, Kate. You're going to fit in here wonderfully."

147

Savannah made it sound as though she were moving in on a permanent basis instead of spending a weekend on the ranch. Kate found herself trusting in the assurance radiating from the enigmatic woman. There was something about Savannah Black. She seemed to possess a secret knowledge. Her own private crystal ball revealing an uncertain future.

The very idea made freezing cold chills race along Kate's spine.

Chapter Thirteen

"Which one of you brain surgeons came up with this idea?" Jesse glanced between Brock and Riley and fought to restrain his amusement. "Damn sure Van wasn't involved in this one."

"Van's become boring since she got knocked up."

If he wasn't familiar with Riley and the man's warped brand of humor, Jesse might have been put off by the comment.

"You're supposed to be the sensible one," he said, raising an eyebrow at Brock. It was hard to believe the man who was usually the voice of reason bought into the madness.

"Give it up, Jesse. I can tell you're jonesing to try these bad boys out."

Duh! Of course he was. The power jumpers, or souped up stilts, were deceptive in their simplicity. At first he'd thought the three foot long contraption was some kind of mutated slingshot. They'd had him sit down on a hay bale and strapped them on. One set of straps secured the device below his knees. The curved metal strip arched behind his calves and more straps fastened over his boots, clamping him down into an L-shaped bracket. The whole thing made him feel strung tight as an arrow stretched along a bow in preparation of being shot through the air.

Jesse hadn't expected to be able to stand on the jumpers, but found it easy to balance on the slender stilt-like toy. He made a few tentative movements, shifting his weight from the balls of his feet to his heels. The jumpers bounced similar to being on a pogo stick.

He rolled his weight from heel to toes, pushed off slightly and nearly lost his head. Quite literally. The power jumpers sprung and shot him straight up in the air toward the loft. Jesse saved himself from sustaining a head injury by putting his arms out to keep from plowing head first into the hard wood.

"Som' bitch," he hollered.

He bounced a few more times before coming to a rest. Brock and Riley were laughing and he could no more stop the devilish grin from curving across his lips than he could stop the sun from rising.

"Game's on. Who's playing?"

"Yeehaw!" Riley hooted. "Just gotta find us a fourth first."

"Van's out and no way will Cord play," Brock chimed in. "Tam and Steph wouldn't even consider it. Craig and Sandy..." He shook his head. Words were not necessary, they all understood. The Morton's had yet to embrace the extreme games common place to the Shooting Star Ranch.

"Zeke needs to quit that damn school and get his ass back here."

"Um...sure. Barring such a drastic event happening in the next few minutes, we'll have to find someone else, Riley."

Too bad Tink hadn't joined them for the weekend getaway. She was full of gumption and would probably come up with an even more wild variation of what they had in mind.

Jesse rubbed his jaw, lost in thought. Would Kate be willing to engage in the fun and games? Hell, there was no harm in asking.

"Get these things off my feet." He carefully sat down on the hay. "I'll do some fast talking and see if Kate will play. You two get everything ready to go."

"The city girl? No way." Brock stood with his arms crossed over his chest. "Hell will freeze over before Miss Priss will come out and play."

Jesse punched Brock in the arm, wincing at the pain shooting through his hand. Damn cowhand was built solid. "Jackass! Don't be fooled by the exterior. There's a wildcat lurking within that shined up city girl." He stared pointedly at Brock. "You experienced some of her fire firsthand. Do you doubt she can hold her own?"

"Hell no. She's a firecracker all right."

"Hey!" Riley had stopped laughing. His brow crinkled and a pout formed on his lips. "Exactly what the fuck happened down there in Denver?"

Brock slapped him on the back none too gently. "You missed out is what happened."

"Well, fuck. You better be coming up with some details pretty damn quick."

"Maybe next time I invite you to take a road trip, you won't turn me down." Brock's smug smile said it all.

80

Talk about bizarre. Kate had never seen anything remotely close to the odd sight which greeted them in the ranch yard. Brock and Riley, two grown men, wore stilts strapped to their boots and were bouncing around performing aerial feats. Riley hurtled into a stunning back flip while Brock made a huge leap over the bed of someone's pickup truck. The two of them were

151

making jumps up to nine feet long and seven feet high.

Oh, man. She was anxious to try them out. It was a good thing she'd changed into a T-shirt and capris.

Riley moved next to her, bouncing from one foot to the other. "Wanna play, little girl?"

"Back off," Jesse warned. He'd picked up a wicked-looking pair of paintball guns and handed them to the two men along with goggles and ammo packs. Once his friends had their gear squared away, he turned to her holding a pair of the stilts.

"How about it, Katie. We need a fourth. Want to play?"

"Hell yes!" As if there was any chance she'd turn him down. "Gear me up, baby."

"Yeehaw!"

Kate hid a secret grin. She had an advantage the guys knew nothing about. More than ten years of gymnastics classes made her limber and perfectly comfortable with high flying aerobatics.

She was going to kick some ass.

They gave her a few minutes to get used to the jumpers, during which she pretended to have a difficult time controlling the springy shoes. Anticipation sped up her heart rate. Kate was going to show these boys a thing or two. They wouldn't underestimate her again.

"How're you doing? Okay?"

"I'm ready, Brock. How about you?"

The over confident cowboy chuckled. "Don't worry, sweetheart. We'll take it easy on ya."

Kate ducked her head and let her hair fall forward to cover her expression. After getting her humor under control, she glanced up at him and spoke in a meek tone. "That's not necessary."

Riley snickered. "Sure it is." Then he turned to Jesse. "Y'all ready?"

"Yup. Rules are there are no rules other than you hurt Kate and we're gonna throw down."

She groaned and bounced restlessly. It was going to be a pleasure to teach these good ol' boys a lesson. "Come on, you sissies. Let's hit it already."

"Whoa. Red's got some fire in her blood."

Brock's teasing words made her itch to show him up. The two teams separated and headed off in different directions. It irritated her how Jesse kept looking over his shoulder to make sure she was keeping up. The jerk!

As soon as he wasn't paying attention, she set off on her own. Her finger tensed on the trigger. Class was in session. Time to hog-tie some cowboys.

"I think they're close."

Kate didn't respond. Jesse looked over his shoulder only to discover she was gone. Dammit. Now he'd have to circle back around and make sure she was all right.

What a shame. Brock and Riley weren't being very stealthy. In fact, they were making enough noise to hide his approach.

He considered the situation briefly and decided the opportunity was too good to let pass by. First he'd score a few points against the guys, then he'd go find his woman.

Jesse knew how to move without making his presence known. He followed their erratic path until he was in a position presenting a clear shot. Crouched behind some scraggly bushes, he took aim and waited from them to get closer.

Brock was in front of Riley. Flexing his finger over the trigger, Jesse held off until the two men separated. He wanted to score hits on both of them and had the patience to make sure it happened.

Riley started to move in a different direction. He gave it a few more seconds, planning to shoot rapid fire then run for the hills. Jesse began a silent countdown.

Three.

Two. Deep breath.

One.

He began to squeeze the trigger, but backed off, startled by a loud and strangely savage war cry.

"Aiyeeeee!"

What the fuck?

The attack was brutal, violent and effective as hell. In a flash of controlled motion, Kate dropped from a branch high in a tree off to his right, screamed and started firing. She scored several hits on both Brock and Riley, bounced, performed an insane rolling twist, then disappeared from sight again.

His two friends grumbled and moaned over the successful strike. Jesse puffed out his chest, feeling amazed and proud of her.

Damn straight. That was *his* fiery woman.

He retreated from the massacre and went looking for Kate, who turned out to be excellent at not being found unless it was what she wanted. He didn't see her until she was hanging upside down from a tree with her paintball gun four inches from his face and aimed directly between his eyes.

"You wouldn't dare."

Then the witch pulled the trigger, the weapon clicking on the empty chamber. She was out of ammo.

Holy shit. Taking a direct hit to unprotected skin from such a close range would have hurt like hell. He couldn't believe the crazy minx had actually tried to shoot him.

"Dammit, Red!" He tried not to, but ended up rubbing his forehead where the paintball would have hit.

"Don't be such a baby. I knew it was empty." A devilish gleam sparkled in her eyes. "Never underestimate the power of a city girl on a mission. And don't dare me if you're not prepared for me to follow through." She burst into hysterical laughter.

Incredible. Jesse was seeing a different side of Kate. There was a fun-loving sprite behind the sophisticated veneer he'd not imagined, but was thrilled to have set free.

By the time Brock and Riley waved the white flag, giving up on the game, both men were covered with red paint. They'd scored two hits on Jesse, but had not been able to touch Kate. She was too cunning and competitive.

After the game, he suggested a tour of the ranch. He found it hard not to laugh at the pained expression which filled her face at the mention of going on horseback. The memories of sore muscles from their last ride must still be too fresh in her mind.

The idea of taking one of the ATVs turned out be a satisfying compromise. Driving over the land with Kate snuggled up close, arms wrapped around his waist, head resting on his shoulder was a little slice of heaven.

He was puzzled over how Millie had known they were headed out for a ride. Maybe the wily old woman had a touch of Savannah's clairvoyance. No sooner had he pulled the ATV out of the barn than she'd showed up with a wicker picnic basket filled with tantalizing treats and a blanket. Kate's sketchbook had been added to the cargo bin and off they went.

Each new sight seemed to delight her, but her visceral response to the piece of ranch land Savannah had deeded to him stirred affection in Jesse's heart. He hadn't even gotten the chance to tell her the land was his. As soon as he stopped, she jumped from the vehicle and spun around.

"This is amazing. Can we stop here for a while? I have to draw this." She didn't give him a chance to respond. Kate snatched up her art supplies and raced across the grassy hilltop.

He knew what she was feeling and seeing, perched upon the amazing vantage point. Looking out to the west in the foreground was one of the most beautiful views of the ranch. The house, foreman's cabin, bunkhouse, stables and corral nestled close together. To the north of the ranch was pasture land, and to the south was the lake, boathouse and the Mortons' cabin. Water in the small river snaking across the property sparkled in the bright afternoon sunlight.

In the background was the spectacular rise and fall of the Rocky Mountains standing sentry along the extreme western border of the ranch. Shades of gold and green covered the land, turning to deep browns as the elevations rose, then stark grays and black until reaching the snow capped peaks.

"I have to draw this," she repeated.

The slight tremor of excitement in her voice touched a place deep in his heart. Jesse moved to the edge of the hill and spread out the blanket. Without a word, Kate sat down, opened her sketch book and became lost in her work.

He set the basket on a corner of the blanket and laid back to watch Kate. A gentle breeze ruffled the tall grass surrounding them and fluttered through her dark red locks, making him think of a lovers caress. Her absolute focus made him feel a bit neglected, but he enjoyed watching the emotions cross her face.

One moment her brow would be crinkled as she determined the best way to capture the image on paper, and the next her eyes would shine over some newly discovered detail. She would mutter to herself or chew on her bottom lip for a few seconds, then her fingers would become a blur of motion.

Page after page became filled with incredible renderings of the land he loved. She filled one with mountains. Another showed an overall image of the property. Kate even drew him sitting on the hill, staring off into the distance. After several hours he made her take a break.

"Come on, honey. Let's have something to eat."

She was reluctant to put down the sketchbook, but a growl from her stomach ended any potential argument.

"Okay," she agreed with a heavy sigh. "I'm losing the light anyway."

They began pulling items from the basket, spreading out a veritable feast. Club sandwiches piled high on homemade honey and sunflower seed bread. Sealed containers of potato and three-bean salad, a jug of lemonade, and dill pickle spears rounded out the menu. Millie had even added two chocolate chip cookies for each of them.

"Tell me about this land? How'd you know about this spot? Is it part of the ranch lands?"

Her interest in the ranch made him feel light as a feather, and Jesse realized he'd been worried what Kate would think of his home. The way her eyes lit up, and her excitement lifted his spirit. While they ate dinner, he answered her questions.

"Savannah left her home because she was bothered by people who found out about her abilities. People began to have expectations, and bombarded her with their bad psychic karma. She packed up her belongings and set off without a clear destination in mind."

Jesse had always been amazed by Savannah's strength. Leaving everything she knew, heading out to carve a place in the world on her own. Living alone on the ranch and hiring four strangers to be there with her.

One day she'd sat them down and explained about her second sight abilities, and how they had guided her choice in hiring Brock, Riley, Zeke and himself from the dozens of applicants for cowhands.

"She drove as if on automatic pilot, drawn to the land. The Shooting Star Ranch is comprised of twenty thousand acres. Basically everything as far as you can see."

He looked out over the ranch, thinking back over the past year. So much had changed in all their lives.

"Tamara owns a bookstore in town. She and Savannah became instant friends, but it took a lot of convincing to get her to move out here. Tamara used to be afraid of snakes, mice, spiders...you name it."

"How did Savannah meet Cord?"

Jesse chuckled as memories of the monumental clashes between the couple played through his mind.

"The place started out as a pleasure ranch. I've told you about some of the wild games we played. Basketball in a muddy meadow on ATV's, extreme jet ski challenges, bizarre relay races only scratch the surface. All the activities were very similar to our paintball challenge earlier.

"Cord was serious, all about the working aspects of the ranch. He wanted things organized and running with precision. Every time we played there was a knock-down-drag-out argument between the two of them. I won't even talk about how Cord reacted to Riley's pranks on Tamara."

It was Kate's turn to laugh. "The stories you told me about the lengths he went to get her attention are hysterical."

He nodded. "But Cord didn't see things that way. He was hired to make things run well, and damned if he wasn't going to make that happen."

There had been a few scary times when tempers had flared. In the end, though, they had all learned to thrive on the ranch.

"Savannah was desperate to tie us all to the ranch. To keep the family she'd built together, the people who loved and accepted her despite her abilities. On the morning of her wedding, she gave Tamara, Brock, Riley, Zeke and me a gift. The deed to ten acres of ranch land for each of us."

Kate's gaze snapped to his. "She gave you ten acres of her ranch?" Her tone was incredulous.

Jesse watched her expression as he spoke, then held his breath waiting for her reaction. "You're sitting in the middle of my land."

With a gasp, her gaze darted around them before returning to focus on him. "This is your land?"

He nodded, unable to speak.

"Jesse," she squealed. "This place is amazing and beautiful. Why didn't you tell me before? I bet you've got tons of plans for when you return from Denver."

It hit him then. Alone. He'd return to the ranch alone. While she may enjoy a brief visit, this was not the life she wanted. Kate's dreams were tied to the city. "What's to tell? I own a bit of land on a sprawling ranch in Montana. You're a city girl. We both know the score."

Kate stared at him for long, drawn out seconds, then scooted over and pushed on his shoulders until he lay back on the blanket.

"Make love to me." The words spoken in a husky tone made his cock rise. He lay still as she straddled his hips and began to unbutton his shirt, confusion warring with intentions. There were so many things he wanted to say, but he was afraid.

Regardless, he was more certain than ever. Kate was the one.

Jesse longed to tell her, to pronounce his love, but the words died in his throat. For now, he decided to wait and see how things went. He had all the time in the world to talk Kate into building a life with him here on his land.

For the first time, he let her take control and they made love. It was slow and tender, almost poetic. Kate teased and tormented until finally sliding down over his cock, enveloping Jesse in the damp heaven of her body.

It could have been the setting sun bathing them in shades of purple and magenta before darkening to black velvet dotted with the bright twinkle of stars. Maybe it was letting Kate set the pace. Or possibly because of the location. Jesse wasn't sure, but he felt as though their souls mingled together. No matter what it was, he was no longer capable of holding back the emotions.

Kate's body tightened, she cried out as her orgasm crested and collapsed against his chest. He wasn't far behind.

"I love you," Jesse blurted as he climaxed.

Her entire body tensed, making him regret the lapse in control. Not the words or feeling, but for putting her on edge. Then he decided hiding was not something he did well. Might as well put his cards on the table.

"This is my home, Kate. I want you to share it with me."

"Jesse." The wheels were turning, fast. He saw it in her eyes as Kate scrambled across the blanket. She dressed quickly, shielding herself from him.

There was no turning back now, but this was the part he'd dreaded. "You knew my time in Denver was limited. When I leave, I'll be coming back here to build a house. Right here on this hill." He rubbed his face with one hand while trying to find the right words. "I love you, and want you by my side."

Quicker than a flash of heat lightning, distance spread between them. Kate's gaze drifted over the darkened land, her fingers knotting together. The reaction confirmed his worst fears. Her heart belonged to her career, and her career was tied to the city. There was no way she'd give up her dreams and move to the middle of nowhere with a two-bit cowboy.

Taking pity on them both, Jesse gave her an easy out. "Don't worry, honey. You don't have to say anything. Just know the offer will be there if you ever decide to live a simpler life with someone who loves you."

Now all he had to do was figure out a way to give them both what they wanted.

Chapter Fourteen

"Hey, wait a minute. That was cool. How'd you do that?"

Kate watched the graphics roll by on the computer screen early Sunday morning. They were all simple stock art and photographs, nothing special. What made the website interesting were the effects Steph had programmed.

"It's a simple bit of coding. That's all," Steph stated, devaluing her genius with computers.

Yeah, right. There was nothing simple about the websites design and function. In fact, Kate found it to be quite ground breaking. The sites Steph had created and maintained for her clients were the best Kate had ever seen. The flow of information and ease of navigation were impressive.

Adding some of her art would make the websites award winners. The two of them together would make an unstoppable team.

She wondered if Steph would consider moving to Denver and combining forces. Instead of Kate Brooks Designs they could form B&B Designs.

Hmm...had a nice ring to it.

"You are a coding goddess," she complimented. "I hate the stuff. Trying to set up a drop-down menu gives me a massive headache. I can't even imagine what attempting something this detailed would do."

Steph wore a wide grin letting Kate know how much the compliment pleased her. "The graphics suck, but the sites are well organized."

A million different ideas buzzed through her mind, but she kept circling back to the same thing. Steph was the laidback kind of woman who was more comfortable behind the scenes. Put her in a boardroom with influential clients and she'd falter.

Actually, it was perfect. Kate thrived on running the show. With a skilled technical person such as Steph behind her, they'd turn the web design world upside down.

The one obstacle was location. Steph was happy on the ranch. She enjoyed being close to her brother and friends. And with a niece or nephew on the way... Convincing her to move would be next to impossible. She gave it a shot anyway.

"Any chance of you leaving the ranch and moving out to Denver?"

Steph appeared confused. "Why would I want to move?"

"We'd make a great team. With my art and your designs, we'd be a huge success. Create our own company. Set our own rules. Be our own bosses. Become rich and famous."

"I'm already my own boss, and I have no desire to be rich and famous." She thought about it for a moment before adding, "Well, rich maybe. Fame is overrated."

Damn. "What about getting out from under big brother's thumb?"

Uh-oh. Wrong thing to say. Steph's brow crinkled, her lips thinned, and her eyes burned a hole through Kate.

"I enjoy being here with Cord. He's a great brother. Ranch life suits me."

Kate nodded. "Sorry. I got carried away. I didn't mean to

offend you."

Steph closed out the website they'd been viewing. "It's okay. No harm done."

No harm and no headway either. Kate wandered outside and sat on the porch swing to think.

What about Jesse's offer? The question whispered through her mind.

Jesse's offer. The man had thrown her for a loop. Sure, she had strong feeling for him. Hell, she loved him. But give up her career and move out here with him?

If I did, then I'd be free to start my own business with Steph as a partner.

True. It didn't really matter where the boardroom was. If they had their own company, they didn't need one anyway. Times when a meet and greet with the client was necessary, travel was an option. The airport wasn't too far away. Kate could go to the client's boardroom.

But how steep would the cost be?

Working from the ranch would mean putting more focus on Jesse. It would be the equivalent of scrapping her goals, dreams and ambitions. He had not offered marriage.

This brought her back to the bigger issue. Why did his declaration of love freak her out? Yes, people often said things in the heat of the moment and didn't mean it. She didn't feel this was the case. Jesse meant every word. Felt deep emotions for her.

The ranch was his life. His home. If she pleaded and begged, he'd probably move to Denver, but to what ends? He wouldn't be happy in the city. While she'd still have her career on track, they'd both be miserable. They'd grow apart and eventually he'd leave.

What if she sacrificed her career? Would she have regrets down the road? If she did, it would come between them for sure.

What would I truly be giving up?

She made a mental list of the things she'd no longer have to deal with. Stress—this was a biggie. Uncomfortable dress clothes. Painful high-heeled shoes. Riesman. Struggling for recognition.

The connections and contacts she'd made in the business world would still be there. Location would be different, but so what. One of the beautiful things about being a graphic artist is the ability to work from anywhere you desire.

But she'd lose the part of the job she loved. The power lunch meetings and designer suits, high-pressure presentations, awards and recognition. Having her own business and being the woman in charge of the many employees working under her. It would be hard to walk away from the high she got by being part of the seductive world of Denver's business elite.

What would I gain?

Kate listed the potential benefits. Being with Jesse. Living on the ranch and having fun. Working with Steph. Creating a business they'd both be proud of. Setting down permanent roots. Maybe even plan for a family.

Savannah suddenly appeared at her side. Kate remembered the story Jesse had told of everything the strong woman had given up and the happiness she'd found in return.

The other woman's arm went around her shoulders and Kate's whirlwind thoughts quieted. She experienced a state of calm and serenity from Savannah's touch. It made her wonder if Savannah had other abilities nobody talked about.

Without any preamble or pretenses, Savannah plunged ahead.

"You're good at being smart and analytical. Determining the best path through detailed planning. How far has that gotten you? What do you have holding you to your current life?"

Good question. What did she have?

Savannah answered for her. "You have a career in a company which will not go anywhere. To achieve your dreams, you need to strike out on your own. Denver is a place. You have no family there. Only one close friend. I see Tink giving it up in a heartbeat for the right man. Then what's left?"

Tink? Holy shit. How did she know about Tink?

"Focus, Kate. Forget trying to intellectualize everything. Follow your heart. Look inside your soul and see what is most important. Having a demanding career and being alone, or working for enjoyment and being surrounded by love."

She broke the issue down to the most crucial points in her mind. She loved Jesse, his friends, the ranch. She would give up Denver and the lure of power for a low-key version of her dream, but not to merely live with him. He had to be willing to give everything in return.

It had not been important to her before Jesse, and it might sound old fashioned, but she wanted what Savannah had— marriage and family. She couldn't accept less.

Letting go and standing, Savannah stared into her eyes. Kate felt as if the clairvoyant woman saw straight into her private thoughts and emotions.

"Your heart won't lead you astray."

No, but it may get stomped on along the way.

Kate snapped out of her stupor when the screen door slapped against its wooden frame. She looked around and had to wonder if she'd been daydreaming.

જી

It was another gorgeous afternoon with the sun shining and a light breeze keeping the temperature from climbing too high. This time Jesse talked Kate into a short horseback ride out to the lake after lunch. The sparkling water reflected the brilliant amber, gold and rust leaves of the trees, which were decked out in dazzling fall colors. The season had arrived in Montana early.

Spreading out the blanket in the spot she chose, Jesse sat with his back resting against a large tree trunk.

"C'mere, honey."

She moved into his body, cradled between his legs, and stared out at the water. It was hard to believe they'd been together such a short time. The emotions running between them were stronger than anything she'd ever felt before.

His clean masculine scent wrapped around her, making Kate's heart thud against her ribs. As they settled into a comfortable silence, her thoughts returned to fretting about the future.

"You're thinking too much, Katie." He kissed her temple. "Relax. Be happy and have fun. Everything will work itself out one way or another in time, whether you worry over it or not."

Funny, smart, playful—everything she'd longed for in a man. He was dominant in the bedroom, but not domineering, allowing Kate to make her own decisions. And being with him out here on the ranch was different. They were different. Somehow better and fitting together in a new, easy-going way.

Questions without any clear answer bombarded her once again. She tried to push them away, but her focus was shot. Eventually, she moved across the blanket and sat facing Jesse.

Contemplating the man she loved.

Something held her back from saying the words. Yesterday she'd shown him by making love on his hilltop. The words hadn't been necessary then. They'd spoken with their bodies, shared a deep mating of souls.

Today she wanted to capture the intense emotions turning his amber eyes into a deeper whisky brown. To draw the beauty she saw beneath the rugged cowboy exterior.

"Take your shirt off."

Without a word, Jesse took off the Stetson, which seemed to be a part of him, and pulled off his faded T-shirt.

"Now put the hat back on."

Gorgeous. He leaned back against the tree, hat pulled down low over his eyes, his muscular, tanned torso glistened in the sunlight. Long legs were stretched out, one booted ankle crossed over the other.

She leaned forward and made a minor adjustment to the hat. The shadow falling over his face was good, but she wanted to connect with his expressive eyes.

Kate's fingers flew across the paper as if the devil were chasing them. Page after page, she struggled to bring out what she saw in him. Even though it was some of her best work, the drawings all fell short of revealing the many facets of his larger-than-life spirit or the depth of emotions he stirred within her.

The hard masculine planes and angles were easier to depict. She'd never grow tired of the subject matter, but studying his body whet her appetite to satisfy other cravings. Carnal hungers she'd discovered only with him.

He had not fucked her ass again, and she longed for a repeat of the explosive passion. It had been a profound sexual awakening for Kate. The sensitive nerve endings he'd brought to life began to tingle as she remembered her tight channel stretching around his thick shaft. The heady rush of him powering into her very soul.

She felt a desperate need to repeat the encounter. Right here. Right now.

Closing the sketch book, she set it aside, giving him a come-hither glance from beneath her eyelashes.

"What do you need, honey." He seemed to have no problem reading the urgency in her eyes. Sensing her reluctance, his next words were spoken in a deeper, commanding tone. "Tell me."

Those two words, spoken with unquestionable authority, freed Kate. He was the one man with the ability to vanquish the independent and in charge woman. Capable of allaying all fears and relieving her of any responsibility. He would ensure her pleasure, multiple times, before seeking his own. It wasn't her job to provide his enjoyment. Jesse would take care of them both. All she had to do was hand over the reins.

Oddly, relinquishing all burden and obligation to him made Kate feel empowered.

"I want you to fuck my ass. Hard."

He stared into her eyes, appearing to search for something. Then he nodded. "Strip." Jesse's gaze traveled down her body and back up again, leaving her skin feeling tight. "Slowly."

She waited for apprehension to strike, but it didn't happen. It didn't matter if anyone saw them, or that they had no lube. There was no need to be concerned. He'd keep her safe and make it good. She trusted in him.

Her fingers trembled with anticipation as Kate released each button and let each piece of material fall to the blanket. He was going to fuck her ass. Give her pleasure beyond description. Take her on a whirlwind trip to the heavens.

After kicking her panties aside, Kate turned and positioned herself on her hands and knees. Jesse had other plans for them.

"Uh-uh, Katie. On your back. I want to watch your face as I ream that gorgeous ass."

She gasped, hot juices sliding over her swollen labia. He wanted a repeat of the first time and the intimacy only possible when facing your lover. Good!

He waited for her to follow his instructions, still leaning casually against the tree, but there was nothing casual about his expression. He looked fierce, a predator sizing up its next meal.

A tremor shook her and she whimpered, waiting for his next move.

Jesse peeled off his boots and socks. Maintaining the intense eye contact, he rose and shucked the jeans. His cock sprang free, grateful to have escaped its imprisonment, and bobbed a hello.

The tip of her pink tongue licked across her lips in invitation. Her mouth was a tempting distraction—an inescapable lure.

Straddling her chest, he fed Kate's eager mouth. Lips stretched wide, she sucked him hard, taking his cock to the back of her throat. He moaned, head falling back, lost in the feel of her tongue swirling around his length.

He thrust slow and easy until her hand cupped his balls. She massaged the tight globes, one finger reaching back to stroke over his perineum, externally stimulating his prostate.

"Fuck," he gasped and pulled back. "Keep that up and you won't get the ass reaming you deserve, honey."

Lust-filled eyes watched closely as he scooted backward,

stopping when his knees bracketed her hips. Her luscious tits and puckered nipples merited diligent consideration.

Moans and whimpers passed her reddened lips as his fingers tweaked, plucked and strummed the firm peaks then soothed the quivering flesh with his tongue.

"Are you wet for me?" Instead of waiting for an answer, Jesse devoured her breast, suckling firmly on her nipple.

Kate arched beneath him, hips bucking wildly. "Yessss," she cried. "Please, Jesse. Fuck me."

Not one to disappoint, he drifted farther down her body, cock waltzing along her engorged clit. He moved to her side and her eyes flashed daggers at him. Wrapping his hands around her thighs, he placed both legs over his left shoulder, lifting her ass from the blanket.

Without preamble or warning, he thrust his fingers into her slick pussy, lingering briefly before pulling out and veering toward the constricted pucker below. Her arousal provided the perfect lubrication, and Jesse took great care in preparing her. Kate may enjoy a smidgen of pain to spice things up, but he would not inflict harm. He stretched and lubed her ass, delaying until she rode his fingers, begging for his cock.

Upon finally dipping into her snug passage, he cussed a blue streak. Strong muscles clamped down, rippled along his shaft, and summoned him deeper.

He heard the sounds of someone approaching. Riley's voice intruded a moment later.

"Hey, Jess. We hosed down the north pasture. You two want to play..."

Whatever else he'd intended to say died on his lips when he caught sight of them making love.

Kate grabbed at the blanket in a futile attempt of covering

herself. It was too late. Riley had already gotten an eyeful and hell if Jesse was able to stop. Her wiggling created delicious friction he was powerless to ignore.

"Hands by your head," he ordered. He saw the reluctance in her eyes. "Do it or I'll stop fucking you and let Riley spank this delectable ass."

She dropped the blanket, hands shooting up to her head. The motion propelled her breasts upward and drew both his and Riley's gaze to the bobbing spheres.

"Oh. You're already playing." Riley devoured Kate with his eyes. "Mind if I join in."

"Yes, I do mind. She's mine. You can watch, but no touching," Jesse snarled.

"Aww, man. Come on. It's never been a problem before."

Damn, Riley and his mouth. Kate's gaze shot to his, eyes full of questions he didn't know how to answer.

Riley nodded, his gaze caressing each curve, stopping at the point where their bodies joined. The other man watched the glide of flesh against flesh. The pull and drag of her tight hole gripping his invading shaft.

"Oh my," Kate gasped. Her eyes widened, gaze trained on Riley as he took his cock in hand and began masturbating. The scene was reminiscent of the night they'd watched the movie with Brock and gave him a voyeuristic treat. Jesse had granted Brock a minimal participation, allowing the other man to stroke her clit to climax.

He knew Riley would jump at an offer of the same opportunity. It wasn't happening this time. Not anymore. The longer he was with Kate, the more possessive he felt. Sharing, even in a small way, was not a possibility. There was no time anyway. He was almost there.

Kate's head thrashed from side to side as he continued to fuck her with Riley watching. She tried to thrust, however the position hindered her effort. Reaching around her hip, Jesse stroked her pulsing clit. Her muscles spasmed, convulsed. She screamed.

Riley groaned, shooting come over his hand.

Jesse was sucked along with them, pumping his seed into Kate's ass. He pulled out slowly, lowered her legs, and collapsed in a sweaty heap.

Riley muttered, "Hell of a lot more fun than what I had planned."

Chapter Fifteen

"We hosed down the north pasture."

Riley's oddball comment seemed to come out of nowhere. The meaning of the statement was eluding Kate's sex fogged mind. She turned to Jesse. "What the hell was he talking about?"

"The north pasture is relatively flat ground. Not much grass. It's where we go mudding," he explained.

"Ah." Stories and snapshots of them all covered in mud broke through the haze. Physical exertion. After bone-melting fucking. Not happening. At least not before she got some caffeine and rested. A nap might even be in order.

"What's the deal with no touching or sharing?" Riley grumbled.

She would have ignored him, but Jesse's entire body tensed. His gaze shot to the other man. His voice was full of menace, spoken through clenched teeth. "Not now!"

Okay, that was more effective than any massive dose of caffeine. Alarm bells clanged in her head. She probably didn't want to know what secret Jesse was trying to keep. Rising up on her elbows, she glanced from one man to the other. A weighted silence hung over them.

Throwing caution to the wind, she said, "Now's as good a

time as any. What's going on?"

Riley sprung to his feet. "I...um..." He searched for a valid excuse. "Gotta go tell Brock the game is on hold 'til later." He wasted not a second getting out of there.

Jesse mumbled unintelligible comments under his breath and started getting dressed. His obvious reluctance to talk about whatever it was strengthened her determination to uncover the big mystery.

"You gonna get dressed?" he asked without making eye contact.

"Nope. I want to know what just happened. What was he talking about, Jesse?"

Still not looking at her, Jesse moved over to the horses. He stalled by tightening the cinch straps and readying the animals for the short ride back to the stables.

"Fuck!"

Finally he turned to face her, but his line of vision focused somewhere to the left of Kate's shoulder.

"It's ancient history. No big deal. The boys and I used to share a woman. Riley was testing the waters to see if I'd let it happen with you." He scrubbed at his face. Then his fingers weaved through his hair, messing it up in ways their recent frolicking had not managed.

They shared a woman? All four of them.

"Exactly what does that mean and how is it no big deal?" She reconsidered what he'd said. "Who was it?"

Jesse crouched down in front of her. "We did some experimenting with ménages. It's old news."

Experimenting with ménages. Dayum!

"Who?"

A muscle in his jaw ticked and he appeared to be in pain.

175

Good! He deserved to suffer.

"You not wanting to confess makes me wonder if it's someone I've met. Someone here on the ranch."

"There's no point to this," he grumbled in irritation.

"Fine!" Of course it wasn't fine. She stood and started getting dressed. Knowing would be torture, but not knowing was pretty damn miserable too. Perhaps she was being unreasonable. It was part of his past. Still, it wouldn't let go of her.

"I'm walking back. Alone. When you're ready to talk, come find me." Turning her back on him, she started to walk away.

"Kate," he implored.

She didn't look back. Didn't respond. With her shoulders squared, spine straight, she put on a casual attitude. By the time she reached the house her lip hurt from being gnawed on and Kate was no closer to figuring out why his past was breaking her heart.

ဢ

"I had a life before I met her. What the fuck is wrong with that?" Jesse griped. "She had a life too, but you don't see me hounding her about past sexual partners."

He wanted to lash out. Punch the wall. Kick something.

Everything had been smooth sailing until dumbass Riley had to open his big mouth. And now Dakota stood in the bunkhouse listening, all calm and composed. Usually, Jesse found the man's tranquil demeanor comforting. This wasn't one of those times.

"You didn't have any problems accepting Tamara's wild

past. The sharing had stopped before you two met and meant nothing to your relationship."

Dakota had handled her previous relationship with the ranch cowboys the way he handled everything else. He let sleeping dogs lie instead of stirring them up.

"Did you explain the relationship to Kate?"

Explain it? How was he supposed to explain having shared a woman with his three best buds? Would it be better to wait until after Kate had a meltdown to tell her the woman in question was Tamara.

"There's no way to explain it. She's gonna be pissed. Jealous."

Dakota's expression didn't change. His black eyes held an infinite wisdom beyond his years. Jesse had come to trust the stoic Indian's advice.

"Have you told her you love her yet?"

"Yes."

The other man's eyes narrowed on him, making Jesse feel trapped.

"At a time when you weren't having sex?"

Damn it! He hung his head. "No."

Dakota nodded and bluish undertones in his long black hair shimmered. "Then she doesn't believe it. Women don't trust declarations made in the heat of the moment. Rightly so."

"What's one thing got to do with the other?" Jesse was getting frustrated with the conversation.

"Everything! If she knows and trusts in your love then the past is nothing to be jealous of. If she's secure in your feelings for her, the rest is easier to take." He sighed deeply. "It will still be a bitter pill to swallow, but one she'll be able to get past if she can put her faith in you."

Jesse was a big enough man to admit when something was right, and there was no disputing the logic in what Dakota said. It was time to have a serious talk with her.

The door swung open and Tamara strolled into the bunkhouse all cool and confident, as if she owned the place. The effect on Dakota was transforming. His serious expression lightened. Jesse swore he felt a shimmer of the love radiating between the two of them whenever they got within close proximity of the other.

"What are you boys doing inside on such a beautiful day?"

Each movement was a calculated seduction Dakota's gaze devoured. She sidled up to him, running burgundy polished nails over his chest. Something wasn't right. The tricky minx was up to something. Jesse felt it in his bones.

The couple shared a sizzling kiss, almost swallowing each other's faces. It was disgusting the way she had Dakota wrapped around her fingers, but he didn't seem to mind. In truth, he appeared to relish the experience.

"Oh, hi, Jesse," she purred when she finally quit sucking Dakota's face. "Been looking all over for you."

Yup, she was up to no good all right. He didn't want to ask, but did anyway. "What for?"

The most evil, wicked grin spread over her lips, curling up one side of her mouth. She was definitely stirring up trouble.

"Riley and Brock are playing in the north meadow."

"Yeah. So what?"

It was coming, but she'd make him wait for it. Drag out the suspense. When she was good and ready, Tamara would drop whatever ticking bomb she carried.

"They got it all hosed down nice and muddy."

She paused again, and he wanted to shake her. Make her

get to the point.

"Got a couple of inflatable pool floats hooked up to the horses and they're racing around in the muck." Revulsion was obvious in her pinched expression.

He couldn't wait any longer. He shouldn't ask. Shouldn't fall into her trap. As always, he walked straight into it, eyes wide open. "Who's riding the floats?"

"Steph's there. Got her bikini on."

He gritted his teeth, waiting through another pregnant pause.

"Oh, and Kate's out there too. She has the cutest, tiniest white thong bikini." The grin widened. "Well, it was white."

"Fuck!" He didn't need to hear anymore. "Goddamn Riley." The bastard was deliberately bating him. And here he was swallowing it, hook and all.

Tamara's laughter followed him out the door, along with Dakota's chastisement for goading him. Jesse ignored it all as he stormed to the barn and jumped on one of the ATVs, visions of running down one interfering cowboy racing through his mind. Or better yet, he'd make a noose and hang the bastard from a tall, sturdy tree.

The ride to the pasture seemed to take forever, even though it was only a matter of minutes. When he got there, Jesse let the ATV idle and stared at the insane scene.

Savannah stood off to the side, rubbing her rounded tummy, complaining to Mandy about not being able to play because of being pregnant. Mandy was equally agitated at not being allowed to participate because her daddy would kick some cowboy ass for endangering his daughter.

Brock and Riley raced across the muddy ground. Trailing behind the horses, Steph and Kate held onto the rafts, screaming and laughing. The difference in the shape of their bodies was the only way he was able to determine which woman was who. Both women were covered in mud from head to toe.

He cringed when Kate lost her grip and was flung from the raft, tumbling and careening across the meadow. Fear squeezed his heart in a tight grip as Jesse raced to her side. If she was hurt... He didn't even want to consider it.

Kate jumped up and shook, slinging mud everywhere. A thick coat of the brown sludge obliterated her fair skin, glistening in the sun. The bikini was all but invisible. Fuck if she didn't look sexy, slick and naked. He wanted to lay her down on the ground and fuck her almost as much as he wanted to shake some sense into her.

He was starting to understand why Cord got so upset when Savannah indulged in the wild games they loved to stage.

Kate was bent over laughing, using her hands to sweep the mud down her legs. Jesse wanted to scream. His cock was harder than a steel spike behind his zipper as wet hands grazed over long, toned muscle.

He raced forward, skidding to a halt next to her, the tires slung more mud onto her legs. When Kate noticed him, she smiled and he almost laughed at the sight of her bright white grin peeking out from behind all the muck.

"Hey, baby. You've gotta race me next."

Jesse bit the inside of his cheek to keep from saying anything he'd regret later. "Get on," he ordered.

Kate gave him the most bewildered look. "I'm all muddy."

Mentally counting to ten didn't help. Gritting his teeth, he said, "Get on. Now."

She jumped onto the seat behind him, wrapped her filthy arms around his waist and made a point of rubbing up against his white shirt. This time she was going to get the punishment she deserved.

He drove over to where Brock and Riley sat atop the horses. Not a smudge of dirt had touched them. Sensing his anger, both men tensed up, preparing for a confrontation. Hell if he was going to be so predictable.

Gunning the engine, he spun the ATV, sending a filthy tidal wave in their direction then kept on going. The horses whinnied and the two cowboys cussed up a storm behind him. Kate's grip around his abdomen tightened.

"Hey, where are we going? I was having fun."

Jesse remained silent until he drove behind the bunkhouse and helped her off the vehicle. He led her to the corner where they'd installed an outdoor shower for just such occasions.

Heedless of getting dirty, he pressed her into the wall, molding them together from shoulder to knee. Her hands swept down to his ass, fingers digging into his cheeks as she ground her pelvis against his straining shaft.

"First, your punishment." He kissed her hard, stealing any protest she might have voiced along with her breath. His fingers wound through her damp hair, angling her mouth and holding her in place as he devoured her mouth.

They were both gasping for air when he pulled back. Kate's world twisted and spun until Jesse plopped down on a bench. Before she got her bearings back, he flipped her again. Now she lay across his lap, head hanging down, blood rushing to her face. She began to struggle, but he placed on arm over her back.

"What the hell..."

Her words were cut off, replaced by a screech as his palm landed a stinging swat to her ass. He landed several blows in succession to each cheek. She was shocked to find the blistering heat in her ass spread into her pussy, which swelled, gushing liquid arousal.

Something was seriously wrong with her. She was getting turned on by being spanked. Good Lord.

His hand caressed her ass, soothing inflamed skin and increasing her internal temperature.

"If Mandy hadn't been watching, I would have fucked you right there in the meadow. In front of everyone."

His voice was gravely, filled with sexual urgency.

"Mmm. We're alone now, cowboy. Nothing to stop you from fucking me. Hard." She shifted, grinding her clit on his thigh.

"Not yet, dirty girl."

He landed a few more sharp smacks to her ass and her world spun again. Jesse carried her back to the corner and held her body pinned to the wall. He reached up and Kate screamed as freezing cold water poured down over them both.

"Dammit, Jesse. That's fucking cold."

His hands coasted over wet skin, rubbing away the dirt and bringing back the aching need. She tore at his jeans, popping the button and raking the zipper down. Kate had to have him skin to skin, cock to pussy, in the next few seconds or she'd die. They both grappled with the damp denim, tugging and pushing it past his ass and setting his cock free.

Frantic with need, he grabbed the tiny bikini bottoms, yanking them down her legs. Without any preamble, he lifted her by the hips and slammed Kate down over his length, impaling her with his shaft.

"Ohhh. Fuck yeah," she gasped. Her legs wrapped around his trim waist, ankles crossing above his clenched ass. She tried to move, but he held immobile.

"Jesse!"

"Easy, honey."

"Fuck easy. I want raw. Hard. Fast."

Her words had the desired effect. Jesse roared and began slamming into her. The rough hewn wood scraped her back, but she didn't care. Wet skin slapped wet skin. He took her mouth in a bruising kiss. Staking a claim and showing the possessiveness he felt. They fucked hard, two wild animals in a primal rut.

"Jeez, these two fuck more than rabbits."

Kate didn't search out who'd spoken. She knew Brock's voice by now.

"Damn! Makes me horny as hell," Riley grumbled.

Jesse didn't falter or slow his rapid pace. He broke their kiss long enough to say, "Go find your own woman." Then his lips were sealed over hers again, tongues twining and she was lost.

The two cowboys said something else, but she didn't pay them a bit of attention. Everything disappeared from her mind other than Jesse's hard body, plundering mouth and thick cock drilling into her quivering pussy.

With each thrust, he bent his knees and powered forward, the head of his cock hitting her sweet spot. When she came, Kate screamed, unconcerned who heard. Everything that mattered was within her grasp.

Chapter Sixteen

"When are you coming home?" Cord asked as they sat at the big table eating one of Millie's magnificent feasts that evening.

Good question. Jesse paused with the fork halfway to his mouth. It all depended on Kate and how quick she worked magic with her art.

"I'm not sure. Depends how long it takes Kate to finish her work on Mastering Life."

"Hmm. I should be done in a week, two tops."

Kate's casual tone, coupled with the words, stopped his heart and stole his breath. The conversation continued around him while Jesse fought off a panic attack.

"Wow, that's great," Savannah said. "You can be home by the end of the month then."

He wanted to deny the possibility. Find a wrench to throw in the works and slow things down. The thought of leaving Kate left him feeling empty.

"Good. We need the help around here with Zeke gone off to school," Brock stated.

The rest of the meal passed in a daze. Jesse nodded his head and mumbled at the appropriate times. His thoughts were on how to get Kate back to the ranch. Permanently.

After dinner he took her out to the porch swing for some privacy. With one arm wrapped around her shoulders, he tried for a relaxed attitude but tension filled him.

"Are you having a good time here, Katie?"

Her answer was quick and sure. "Absolutely! Everyone's treating me like family, and I love not having to worry about deadlines and meeting times."

"Good. I'm glad you feel comfortable here." He took a deep breath, forming his next question with care. "What about coming to live here with us once your work for Mastering Life is done? Have you thought anymore about my offer?"

Her legs stopped swinging, and she turned to stare at him. Jesse's heart lodged itself in his throat as her eyes assessed his expression.

"What's the deal? There has to be more to this? Are you asking me to give up my career and move out here?"

"No." He shook his head. "I don't want you to give up anything."

Her brow creased as she thought about it. "I'm confused, Jesse. Help me out. What exactly are you saying?"

Shoot, he was blowing it, giving her the wrong impression. His nervous emotions and doubts were screwing up what should be simple. He loved Kate. Needed to be with her, yet held his true feelings in reserve. If he confessed to wanting commitment, his ring on her finger and kids, she'd feel pressured. He didn't want her to pull away.

There was no doubt she cared about him, but her goals meant a lot to Kate. She had something to prove, and a better shot at doing so by staying in Denver. He held the thoughts back, not willing to hang himself out to dry if her aspirations for a high profile career meant more to her than he did.

"You wouldn't have to give up your dreams, honey. Think about it. Steph is a wiz with websites. You've got the art covered. The two of you would make a great team. I bet she'd be thrilled to start a business together. Combining your skills would be a guaranteed success."

He caught a flash of something in her expression, like she'd already considered what he'd suggested. Then she turned back toward the yard, staring off into space, lost in thought for what seemed to be an eternity.

"Let me get this straight. You want me to pick up my life and move in with your friends so I can start a business with Steph? Is that the only reason?"

"Aw, honey. You know it's not. I want to be with you. I hate the idea of coming back here and never seeing you again. I love you, Kate!"

"So you're offering...what?"

Fuck. He wasn't handling this conversation very well. Fumbling over words. Struggling to make her understand. "I plan on beginning construction on the house when I get back. I'll add in an office for you to work from. Once it's done we can move in there."

"It's not enough. I want more."

The words were spoken in a whisper, but he heard them loud and clear. He couldn't compete with her career. His anxiety was replaced with anger as his heart broke.

I'm not enough for her. She'd said "it's" but that's not the way it sounded to him. He took the statement differently.

"Not enough?" He shot to his feet, knowing he'd spoken harshly, but unable to calm down. "I'm offering my life. What the fuck more do you need?"

Kate stared at her feet, refusing to meet his eyes. Anger

186

turned to fury. Even if she was thinking of how to answer, Jesse had to put some distance between them before he did something he'd regret.

"Whatever. It doesn't matter."

He was being unreasonable, a total jackass, but her words cut deep. There wasn't much to be done to fix things. It had been a lofty dream. He'd know from the start there wasn't much likelihood of a sophisticated city girl going for a rough and tumble cowboy. He wasn't suitable or even socially acceptable. She belonged with some cultured, affluent city boy.

Always had—always would.

He had not stood a chance.

Kate walked around in the dark for a while before curling up in a lounge chair by the pool. She wasn't into fairy tales and had no need for a knight in shining armor riding a white horse to rescue her. She didn't need to be saved.

What Jesse had offered was nice. An undemanding life living on the ranch, working with Steph. Hell, she'd already come up with the idea of being partners with the woman herself.

He'd offered to make an office for her in the house he planned to build. His words played through her head. *What if I asked you to live here with us...?*

What had he really been offering? Was he asking her to live with him? To continue their relationship?

Living with him wouldn't satisfy her soul. She wanted the permanent connection, and would gladly give up Denver for the right offer. One of marriage.

The night air was crisp and chilly. Kate pulled her knees up into her chest and hugged herself. The cloudless sky was dotted with millions of twinkling stars which seemed to wink at her. Silent sentinels offering to lift her spirits.

In Denver she stayed busy. Her mind didn't have time to wander. She was always working, not giving herself the time to feel the loneliness. Being at the ranch things were different. This was the first time she'd felt alone here since they'd arrived.

"If you listen carefully, you'll hear the great spirit whisper on the wind."

"Good Lord." Dakota had materialized out of thin air, scaring the shit out of her. The man moved without a sound. Not the soft swish of clothing. No brush of his shoes over the ground. He seemed to float through time and space without disturbing even a blade of grass.

"You have many questions. If you will open your heart and spirit, warriors of the past will offer guidance and comfort. Listen to the words of the wind. Read the message written in the heavens. Close your eyes and allow your heart to take control. Take a deep breath and allow nature to fill your senses."

Following his directions, Kate lay back, closed her eyes, and opened herself to the night.

"Love requires a leap of faith. A trust in the connection you share with not only your lover, but with all things. Move past what you see, hear, smell, taste and touch. Your spirit must be at peace to develop a harmony between itself, body, land and sky. When you achieve balance, your spirit will show you the way."

Kate allowed herself to drift. To feel the hum of life around her. The connection between all the things he'd mentioned. After some time her mind cleared and the confusion lifted, leaving her with a feeling of rightness.

Being in love with Jesse had changed her priorities, moving marriage and family above career satisfaction. Maybe marriage would happen in time if she accepted his offer. If she turned him down, she lost any chance of it happening.

"I know what I need."

Opening her eyes, she glanced around but Dakota was gone, having left as silently as he'd arrived. Oh well. At least she knew her heart now.

Jesse's offer was generous only if his heart were part of the deal. He'd said he loved her, but were they words spoken in the rush of the moment or heartfelt? More than a high profile career, fancy clothes or a huge office she wanted to be secure in their love. Their relationship may have developed quickly, but she knew what she wanted.

"Thank you," she whispered to Dakota and the warrior spirits he'd spoke of.

ॐ

The weekend passed by too fast and before Jesse knew it, Monday had arrived and they'd headed back to Denver. It had been a long, restless night sleeping apart from Kate. He was tired, but ready to work things out between them. Lay his heart on the line and hope for a future with his amazing woman.

He'd been taken by surprise to see how well she fit with the Shooting Star Ranch and his friends. The girls had all taken to her right away. Even Tamara had formed a bond with Kate.

Her artwork had been a big hit. A portrait drawn for Mandy had captivated the young girl. The ranch landscape presented to Savannah would be treasured and hung above the mantle.

There'd been no doubt the guys would be drawn to her

fiery, outgoing personality. He understood them wanting, expecting to share her as they had Tamara, but it would not happen. Tamara had not belonged to him, but Red did.

The flight back passed in a silence that gnawed at Jesse. He'd spent all night figuring things out and knew where he went wrong. This was the perfect opportunity to set things straight.

"Honey."

"Hmm." She continued to gaze out the window.

"Kate." He cupped her cheek and gently turned her to face him. "We need to talk. I didn't do well at expressing myself yesterday. I'd like to try again."

She nodded, her beautiful eyes revealing a readiness to hear him out.

"I hate the thought of leaving Denver without you." His fingers lovingly traced the soft skin along her jaw, memorizing every laugh line and curve of her face. "I love you. I want you to be happy and fulfilled, and I think we can have that. Together. On the ranch.

"It may seem like moving to the ranch would require sacrifice, but there is so much to be gained. You were a different person there. Relaxed, happy. Will you consider leaving the hustle and bustle of the city for a quieter, simpler life in Montana...with me?"

She smiled, love shining in her eyes, and his heart melted.

"Thank you," she whispered. After clearing her throat, her voice became stronger. More certain. "I love you, too. I wasn't sure you meant it when you said the words last time. That's what I needed. The offer was empty without your heart involved."

She loves me. Jesse wanted to shout the news out loud to everyone on the plane. Let everyone know she belonged to him.

How he managed to maintain his composure was a true mystery.

Raising the armrest, she scooted over into his lap, resting her cheek against his chest. His heart raced, filled with joy as he cradled her in his arms.

"I don't need a power career if I have your love. I'd already come up with the idea of starting a business with Steph before you mentioned it. Do you think she'll go for it?"

"I think she'll jump at the idea. And even if she doesn't, you can still open your own business and run it from the ranch."

"True." She snuggled closer, softly nuzzling his neck. "I'll put in my resignation tomorrow."

He entertained thoughts of joining the mile high club, but was content to merely hold her in his arms. When they got back to her apartment and had privacy, then he'd make love to Kate. Show her how much she meant to him. He drifted off to sleep feeling better than he had in years.

ℂ

It might not be Monday, but it was certainly Manic. Kate was swamped with work. Pushed up deadlines, a new project, and the constant stream of paperwork overflowing her in-basket. When she finally got the chance to sip at her four dollar cup of gourmet coffee it had turned cold.

D.H. was in one of his moods, bitching and moaning at everyone. He was sure to go into a total tizzy once she handed in her resignation. She made a note on a rapidly expanding to-do list, reminding herself to type a letter.

Tink had stopped by for some girl talk and Kate had had to send her away. She'd have to fill her friend in on the wonderful weekend later, even though Kate was anxious to share her news.

Her lunch break was spent on a conference call with an important client while munching an apple at her desk. It was late in the evening when she was done for the day. Kate gathered her laptop and work to be taken home, picked up her letter of resignation and headed for Riesman's office.

Waiting until he was sure to have left for the night was rather cowardly, but she was in no mood to discuss anything with her boss. He'd rant and rave, further delaying her departure. And Jesse waited at the apartment.

Loaded down with files and her bags, Kate dumped the letter onto D.H.'s blotter and sighed in relief. Thank goodness, no confrontation.

She turned and was almost to the doorway when his leather executive chair spun.

"What's this?" He held up the envelope.

Fuck, she was busted. Kate turned on her heel to face him.

"My letter of resignation." She glanced over her shoulder, gauging the distance to the door. "I've, ah, gotta go. Good night."

Kate did a silent countdown to the pending explosion of temper. For the time being, he was still her boss and she didn't want to burn all her bridges. *Ten...nine...eight...*

He inserted a letter opener into the corner of the envelope and ripped it open as she backed away, clutching the files to her chest. D.H. shook out the piece of paper and began reading, muttering the words to himself.

Four...three...almost to the door. Two...

"What the fuck?"

Damn it. So close and yet so far. She took a deep breath.

"I believe the letter is pretty self explanatory."

His beady little eyes locked on her and a cold chill raced along her spine.

"Come here, Ms. Brooks. Sit down. Let's talk."

Damn, damn, damn. She didn't want to have this conversation.

Kate shuffled over to one of the two chairs, plopped down and stared up. Riesman had taken his Napoleon complex to the extreme. His desk was on a platform, raising it above anyone he met with. She felt like a chastised child whenever she sat before the "throne".

He stared at her for several heart beats. "I was waiting to see if we landed the Campbell's account to have this discussion, but it seems waiting is no longer an option." With his elbows propped on the desk, fingers steepled and chin resting on his fingertips, Riesman sighed heavily.

"Business is increasing to the point I can no longer run things by myself. I was planning on promoting you to Vice President. Just last week, I spoke with an architect about making some changes to the floor plan and creating a larger office for you.

"Of course, the position would also come with a substantial raise, along with bonuses for each client you contract. You would have greater responsibility and also increased authority. And you'd have the final say on all art work."

Kate swallowed hard. Good Lord. He was offering her dream on a silver platter. Everything she'd worked so hard for. If she spent a year or two working as VP for Reisman, opening her own business wherever she chose would be a piece of cake.

"The headhunters are already conducting a search for a qualified assistant for you." D.H. dropped his hands. "Mind if I ask who hired you out from under me?"

An assistant? For her? "I...um. I planned on moving. Was going to start my own business."

Planned? Was going to? Why the hell was she talking in the past tense? As if his offer changed anything. It was a really good offer. V.P., an assistant, bonuses.

Riesman leaned forward and went in for the kill.

"What will it take to keep you here?" He seemed to consider the possibilities briefly. "A company car? I'll call the BMW dealership. You can pick whatever model you prefer. Of course, the position comes with an expense account. You'll have a company credit card for entertaining clients. We might be able to work out a clothing allowance."

Her mind was spinning. How the hell was she supposed to pass all that up? A BMW. She pictured herself zipping along in a midnight blue roadster. An expense account and clothing allowance. Damn, she could do some damage at the stores.

The material things were nice enticements, but the boost to her career... This would bring her everything she'd worked so hard to achieve.

Oh God. It was so tempting.

"Let's pretend I never saw this letter." He folded the paper and stuffed it back into the envelope, then came around the desk. Tucking it into her laptop case, he escorted her to the door. "Go home and think about it. You can give me your answer at the end of the week."

Kate's entire body was numb. Somehow, she managed to stand and walk with him, nodding.

Driving home she began to see things in a different light. Her path had been certain only an hour ago, now...

She was a city girl, through and through. A power player. Kate lived for schmoozing the high profile, influential and elite of the business world. She thrived on power lunches, business suits, wining and dining.

Working as V.P. of a company with the stature of Riesman Designs would open doors she'd not even glimpsed or dreamed of seeing from the other side. If she worked hard, she'd be able to write her own ticket to the stars.

But the cost was high. Jesse would be going back to the ranch soon. He didn't belong here. His dreams were on a breathtaking hilltop in Montana. A piece of property he'd pour his heart and soul into. A place where he'd live a happy, uncomplicated life. Her doubts about the future and what he wanted resurfaced. Could she give up the position Reisman offered on the hope Jesse would want to marry her one day? Would he find someone else?

Moisture pooled at the corners of her eyes, blurring her vision. Kate pulled over into the parking lot of a fast food restaurant as fat tears streamed down her cheeks. The very idea of Jesse with someone else, creating a family with another woman, broke her heart. Some lucky bitch living the life she'd been anticipating.

And yet, in offering his love without commitment, Jesse only gave a piece of himself. She needed it all.

If she didn't go with him, she wouldn't be able to keep him. He would move on with someone else. Kate would have her career, money, prestige... Who would she share it with?

Her heart flip-flopped in her chest. Her stomach turned sour, bile rising in her throat. Think. She needed to stop running in circles and analyze.

Grabbing up her laptop, she locked the car and sat in the noisy restaurant. Over a bitter cup of coffee, she weighed and measured both options, pushing emotions out of the equation.

But emotions were the crux of the problem. She could go

with Jesse, give up her goals for love, and hope one day he'd want marriage. Or she could stay in Denver, fulfill her potential, and hope one day to find a man who loved her enough to give her everything, love and commitment.

When they began turning off lights and asked her to leave, Kate had no clue how long she'd sat on the uncomfortable bench seat. Her ass cheeks were numb. Pins and needles ran up and down her legs. She was bone weary, but at least she'd come to a decision. Now to see it through. That would be the hard part.

Stumbling into her apartment, she noticed the half-filled boxes lining one wall of the living room. Kate didn't turn on a light. God, she'd been so sure that morning. Finding herself with an abundance of anxious energy, Kate had begun packing. Books, nick-knacks, odds and ends. Mementoes and memories. The small things one accumulated after living in one place for awhile.

She didn't even bother to undress before crawling into bed and dragging the covers over her head—shutting out the world. Her mind was not as easy to shut off though. It continued to race. It was pure exhaustion, emotional and physical, which drew her into a dreamless sleep.

Chapter Seventeen

Jesse snatched up his ringing cell phone. "Hello. Kate?"

"You didn't find her?"

Fuck! It was Tink again. He rubbed at aching temples.

"Nope. Scared the shit out of a few people though. Do you have any idea how many cars in Denver look exactly like hers?"

The first one he'd spotted had been parked in a deserted parking lot. The windows were steamed up with a couple inside making out. Well, they were until he yanked the driver's side door open and pulled the unsuspecting guy out onto the pavement.

"Mother fucker. I'll kill you for touching my woman."

His fist had been cocked, ready to strike, when the frightened woman poked her head out. A rather large woman with jet black hair who looked very different from Kate.

He'd apologized profusely. Explaining about his missing girlfriend hadn't gone far toward soothing ruffled feathers either. They'd locked the doors and hauled ass out of there. Not that he blamed them for escaping from his vile temper.

"I'm still getting dumped into voice mail at the office and on her cell phone." Tink heaved a frustrated sigh. "Where the hell is she?"

If only he knew.

He'd driven by Riesman Designs several times. The office was dark and locked up tight as a drum. He'd checked restaurants, clubs and even hospitals. There was no sign of Kate anywhere. The police had told him to file a missing person's report after forty-eight hours.

"This fucking city is too big!"

"I've called everyone I can think of who might have seen her. It's like she stepped out of the office and was abducted by aliens."

Abducted. He wouldn't let his mind dwell on the horrifying possibility. This conversation was useless. All it managed to do was make the pounding in his head and the fear in his gut hurt worse. "I'm going to drive by the apartment again, see if she's gone home."

"This isn't like Kate. She's so responsible. Something has to be wrong."

He wanted to rip the phone apart and yell at her to shut up. He didn't want to consider what might have happened to her in such a huge city. There were some rough areas the police weren't able to get under control. Places where drugs and crime ran rampant.

Tink's words invaded his morbid train of thought. "Call me when you find her, Jesse. I don't care what time it is."

The concern in her voice was evident. He offered a few lame reassurances then disconnected the call, making a silent vow not to rest until Kate was safe in his arms. He said a prayer and continued the search.

Jesse had never experienced such overwhelming fear as what plagued him over the past several hours. His driving was erratic and reckless, veering across lanes of traffic whenever spotting a car similar to Kate's. Then he pulled into the complex only to discover her car sitting in its regular spot as if nothing had happened.

Relief staggered him, stealing the air from his lungs. He raced to the car and placed his hand on the hood.

Not hot, but still warm. She had not been there long.

Quicker than the relief had hit, the anger came back, full force. While he'd been out of his mind with worry, she'd been...what? At a bar? At a friend's house? Sitting somewhere safe chit-chatting. Not once thinking of letting anyone know she was all right.

A flick of his wrist and the cell phone sprung open. He took slow breaths, fighting to be calm.

"Jesse? Did you find her?"

"Yeah. She's home."

"Thank God! Where was she? What did she say? Let me talk to her?"

"I haven't gone up yet. When I do, she's not gonna be able to sit for a week."

"Whoa. Chill out. Hear her out before you do anything crazy."

He didn't say anything.

"Jesse. Promise me."

"Tink, I can't promise anything right now."

"Dammit, cowboy." She was cursing him as he hit the disconnect button, turned off the phone and tucked it away in his pocket. Taking the stairs two at a time, he arrived at her door with a loud roar. His fist struck the thick wooden barrier hard. Repeatedly.

"Kate. Open this fucking door."

He continued to bang and yell. Even when a neighbor opened their door and warily peeked out into the hallway.

"Dude, get a grip."

He howled. The sound was both primal and animalistic. "Mind your own fucking business."

"Okay, asshole. I'm calling the cops. You can deal with them."

Jesse reached the man before the words finished passing his lips. He seized the man by his shirt. "I suggest you go back inside…"

"Jesse?"

Hearing Kate's groggy voice, he let the man go and raced to her side. Her face was red and puffy, eyes swollen. Riotous red curls were snarled and knotted in disarray. The dress she wore was wrinkled, appearing as if she'd slept in it. Jesse was assaulted with fear and anxiety again. He was going to wind up with emotional whiplash before long.

"Jesus Christ, honey. What happened to you?"

Pulling her close, he walked her back into the apartment, kicking the door shut behind them. He guided her toward the couch, but she jerked out of his grasp and turned on him.

"Jesse, I'm in no mood for a middle-of-the-night visit. What do you want?" She stood with her hands fisted on her hips, reminding him of Millie when she was upset.

He needed a freakin' score sheet to keep up with this insane night. The anger was back again. "You've got some explaining to do." Too keyed up to sit, he paced the small space while trying to find some reason in the madness.

"You left work tonight and disappeared. Tink and I spent hours trying to figure out what happened. We called your friends, hospitals. I even went to the police station, Katie."

"Don't. Call. Me. Katie!"

Huh! Talk about confusing.

"My name is not Katherine or anything else which can be shortened to Katie. It's simple. Only four letters. K. A. T. E. Stop calling me Katie!"

Visions of how he'd punish her raced through Jesse's mind. A spanking was not going to be adequate. Maybe he'd tie her wrists to the curtain rod in the bedroom, get his whip, and teach her a lesson she'd not soon forget. Then he was going to fuck her hard, giving no quarter, until he collapsed from fatigue.

"Where were you, *Kate*?" He put emphasis on her name, drawing it out slowly. "What the fuck happened? You can't imagine the horrible scenarios that played through my mind."

"Jesus. I don't answer to you."

She turned on her heel and stormed toward the kitchen, but didn't make it there. Jesse grabbed her arm and spun her around.

"When you're in a relationship with someone, it's common courtesy to let them know if you are going to run off somewhere so they don't worry."

Her face softened the slightest bit, giving him a glimpse of the loving woman he'd thought he knew.

"I'm sorry you worried, but I needed some time to myself. Time to think. Okay."

He scrubbed a hand over his face, struggling not to lose his cool. "No, it's not okay. Not without telling someone. You can't disappear for eight hours, not answer your cell phone, and expect it to be all right."

"Can we discuss this in the morning? I'm tired."

Jesse caught a flash of guilt in her eyes, but it was gone before he was certain of what he'd seen.

"It is morning. And I'm beyond tired, Kate. We'll hash this

out now."

"Don't force the issue, Jesse. Don't make me do this until I've had time to figure out what I'm doing," she pleaded.

Until she had time to figure out...what? Oh, hell no, she didn't say that.

"I'm trying to remain calm, but you're pushing me, honey."

"Ohhh-kay. This conversation is going nowhere. I think you should go."

That's all it took for Jesse to snap. He took a firm hold on both of her arms and backed her into the wall. "You owe me an explanation and I'm not going anywhere until I get it."

Kate wanted to fall into his arms and let Jesse soothe away the pain piercing her heart. And she wanted to offer comfort for the fear, anger and hurt he was going through. But she couldn't. She had to be strong.

"I don't owe you anything. We're not married or even engaged." There she'd said it out loud, no matter how much it hurt.

This was better, for both of them. He'd find a woman able to focus on him rather than career. Someone who didn't need marriage, who'd settle for having only a part of him. She'd be able to live the dream she'd worked hard to achieve. Already, she'd made tons of sacrifices to reach her goals. Jesse would be one more.

She didn't want to give him up, but they wanted different things. Kate had to latch onto this opportunity while it was being offered. There was no predicting if their relationship would have gone anywhere or become permanent. The offer D.H. had extended was guaranteed to launch her career.

"We don't fit, Jesse." He started to protest. Kate placed her fingers over his lips, stopping the words. "You know it as well as

I do. I'm city, you're country. I'm career, you're home and family."

"You love me. I love you. Anything else can be worked out."

If only they stood a chance. "I'm sorry, Jesse. It won't work." She cleared her throat, but the emotion wouldn't leave her voice. "Riesman has offered me everything I've sacrificed and worked my ass off for. I can't pass it up."

He backed off slightly, searching her face for...something. His expression turned hard, and the affectionate eyes she loved went cold.

"You're ending it for money. Giving us up for wheeling and dealing." His tone was incredulous.

They way he said it made her seem unfeeling, a money-grubbing opportunist.

"I'm sorry..."

"No! Don't go there. You're not sorry. Not about a damn thing." He took a step back. Again, she longed to soothe him. He looked older, strained. Kate itched to reach out and comb her fingers through his hair, but he wasn't hers to touch anymore. Couldn't give her the one thing she would put above everything else.

Her heart pounded against her ribs in a wild rhythm. Every fiber of her being screamed and raged, demanding she take it back. Take him back.

"I hope the money and prestige keep you warm at night and prove to be good company."

Kate began to shake. Tears welled up, but she held it together as Jesse turned and walked out of her life. She expected him to slam the door, but he didn't even bother to close it.

As soon as he cleared the doorway, she collapsed, sliding

down the wall. The waterworks started, and she allowed the tears to flow free as her heart shattered. She cried until there were no tears left before locking the door and crawling off to bed.

She'd made her choice, picked her career over having half of the man she loved. Now she'd have to live with the decision.

Chapter Eighteen

"You have to get some down time, Kate. You look like shit!"

"Can't! I've got to finish this."

She knew Tink was right, but it was impossible. D.H. had handed her their biggest client and an insane deadline. For three weeks she'd spent every waking moment working. Exhaustion had come and gone, along with her second wind. Now she was running on pure caffeine and determination.

"And what about Jesse? Have you talked to him?"

Kate leaned over and banged her forehead on the desk. The woman was relentless—one endless, broken record, constantly coming back to the same thing. Jesse.

"No! I told you. Haven't talked to him since the break up." She'd adopted the habit of referring to the horrible night she'd thrown away his love for professional advancement as "the break up". On the morning after, she'd closed the blinds over the sliding glass doors in her bedroom in an attempt to shut out the memories. The blinds had stayed shut since then. If only the memories were as easy to shut away.

D.H. had been all too happy to handle getting final approval from Jesse for the artwork she'd done and sending him on his way. Movers had arrived at the apartment complex the next day. Last week a middle-aged couple had moved into his unit.

"You should call him."

She picked up her head, banged it down two more times, than sat back in her chair. "Tink, I don't have time for this now. Please! These designs have to be finished by eight in the morning and ready for our big meeting with Mister McCarthy from the software company. I can't think about *him* or I won't get anything done."

"Mmm..." Tink all but purred. "I envy McCarthy's wife. The lucky bitch has two gorgeous, successful men catering to her every whim. They live in that huge mansion on the beach. What a life!"

Kate ignored her friend's ramblings. The client's personal life was none of her business. If three consenting adults chose to have a committed ménage relationship, more power to them. At least the conversation had turned away from the painful subject of Jesse.

Normally deadlines motivated and inspired her, but not this time. How the hell was she going to get these messed up graphics polished before the meeting? Her muse had deserted Kate, leaving her with no creativity and piss poor ideas. The fate of her future rested on dazzling the client, and so far she was bombing out.

"You're going to collapse if you don't take a breather soon."

"Tink," Kate snapped. Her temper had been extremely short the past few weeks. "Get the fuck out of my office. I'll breathe, eat and sleep tomorrow. Today, I have to finish this fucking account."

Tink flipped long blonde locks over her shoulder with a sharp flick of the wrist. Kate knew it was a sure sign her friend was irritated, but she wasn't going to stop working and soothe Tink's ruffled feathers. When the door slammed in Tink's wake, she gritted her teeth, turning back to the computer. She'd apologize after landing the account.

The first designs she'd come up with were done in sepia tones and appeared to come from the old west. She didn't need a shrink to tell here where the inspiration had come from. Her mind had been preoccupied with thoughts of Jesse and the ranch. Of course it had been reflected in her work.

Rubbing her hand against the ache in her banged up forehead, Kate tried to concentrate. The client wanted crisp, clean lines. Edgy yet professional. Cutting edge and eye catching. The business was all about computers. Software, hardware and manufacturing.

The picture forming in her mind was totally wrong. Lots of big blue sky and green grass waving in a gentle breeze. A corral made from rough hewn fencing. Horses at play, their manes flying behind them as they raced across the land. A handsome cowboy wearing a Stetson and chaps, twirling a long rope. The vivid images shifted to a bedroom. The chaps and Stetson were now all the cowboy wore as he used the rope to tie her to the bed.

Kate jumped out of her chair and paced the confines of her corporate cage. This was ridiculous. She was a grown woman. A mature professional. Not some lovesick girl. It was fourth and goal. Crunch time.

Jeez. Now she sounded like a football coach.

Tink was right. Grabbing up her purse she marched toward the front door. "Norma, I'll be back in a few hours," she called over her shoulder to the receptionist. "I need some retail therapy."

D.H.'s corporate credit card had been burning a hole in her pocket. A mental walk through her closet justified a trip to the mall. After all, she had to appear put together and businesslike tomorrow for the presentation. This called for a new suit.

A few hours and a couple hundred dollars later, Kate had a stunning green jacket and skirt, along with an ivory lace blouse and new shoes.

It was late when she made it back to the office. All the other staff had headed home for the night. Good! There'd be no distractions. She moved behind her desk and wiggled the mouse to terminate the screen saver while slipping off her shoes.

She glanced up at the monitor and gasped. Someone, probably Tink, had opened up the website for the Shooting Star Ranch. Smack dab in the center of her computer stood Jesse in all his western finery, a huge grin on his face.

Closing the internet program, Kate dropped her chin to her chest and wept.

ℰↄ

Tamara stomped into the kitchen and stared at her friends.

"How long are we going to stand by and let this continue?"

She glanced from one face to another. Brock, Riley and Steph. No answers there. Sandy, Craig, Mandy. No one spoke. Cord and Savannah shared a glance, doing that communicating-with-their-eyes thing which drove her nuts. Millie turned to stare out the window. Dakota moved in behind Tamara, wrapping his arms around her waist in a silent show of support.

"He's up there again, sitting on the fucking hill. All he does is sit there and stare off into space, brooding. He's surrounded by thousands of dollars in building supplies and has yet to pound one damn nail." She shot her most intimidating glare at them. "I have a plan."

A few eyebrows rose at the pronouncement.

"I'm going to need some help. Who's in?" Someone had better speak up or there was going to be hell to pay.

"I am. We have to do something," Savannah said.

Cord's steely gaze turned menacing. "Be careful. You're stirring up a hornet's nest better left alone."

"He's so sad. We have to try." Mandy stood and went toe-to-toe with the huge cowboy. The little girl had some balls. Tamara admired her moxie.

"Mandy," her mother chastised.

"No!" Brock stilled Sandy. "She's right. Let's hear Tamara out. We've sat on our thumbs long enough."

Once everyone was seated around the table, she laid out her plan. "We have to stage a bold and creative intervention. I've rented a cabin..."

જી

Kate ran through the PowerPoint presentation once more, and checked the information packets set before each seat at the table. On a sideboard were champagne, orange juice and various pastries.

Everything was ready except her.

She scrutinized her appearance before the bathroom mirror. No amount of make-up would cover the dark circles beneath her eyes. Thank goodness she'd bought the new outfit and kept it in the car, because running home to change after pulling an all-nighter was not happening.

One hour to go before the rest of the staff and the clients arrived.

Lounging back in her brand spankin' new executive chair, Kate sighed heavily. She had to pull this off. Her normal confidence had gone on a vacation. Lingering doubts and insecurities left her feeling weary. Deciding to try and relax until show time, she closed her eyes.

"You're sleeping!"

Her eyes popped open, and she blinked at Tink.

"I can't believe this. Dickhead is in there running your presentation and you're fucking sleeping."

"What?" She jumped from the chair, scrambling to catch up.

"You heard me. Dickhead is in there closing the deal."

"Fuck!" She frantically tugged her jacket into place. "Do I look okay?"

"You look like shit, but there's nothing to fix it now. Get your ass in there, Kate."

The two of them raced down the hall toward the conference room.

"What time is it? Why didn't anyone come and get me?"

"Hey, I just got here. It's eight thirty. My guess is D.H. is taking credit for your work."

"The rat bastard!"

Okay, she had to play this cool. Plastering a fake smile on her face, Kate breezed into the room.

"Good morning, gentlemen. Sorry I'm late." She glanced at the large wall-mounted screen to see where they were in the presentation. "Thanks for your assistance, Mister Riesman. I'll take over now."

You could have heard a pin drop in the deadly quiet room. Her gaze flew to the client, and she gasped. *Holy shit!* Someone might have warned her. The two men were drop dead gorgeous and damn near mirror images of the other.

Both were large, thickly-muscled men. Each had a shock of jet black hair, dark chocolate eyes, and dimples bracketing sensual mouths. Tink was right, their wife was one lucky woman.

"Mister McCarthy. Mister Lundy," she said, nodding toward both men. She was glad they sat together since she didn't know what name went with which man. "As you've already seen..."

She was peripherally aware of D.H. standing, but ignored his movements until he grabbed her arm, spinning her around to face him.

"You are interrupting an important meeting, Miss Brooks. Please leave."

Leave? Fuck no!

"Interrupting. I don't think so. This meeting should not have begun without me here."

"Since the clients are viewing my designs and presentation, your presence is not needed."

Pure evil rolled off Riesman in waves which threatened to suffocate her. Kate refused to be steamrolled. She laughed, but the sound held no humor.

"Nice joke, Mister Riesman, but everyone knows you have no artistic talent." Lowering her voice, she growled the next words. "You're not cutting me out of this."

His gaze shot to the client and he held up a finger, asking for a moment. Then he tried to drag her from the room. Kate wasn't about to leave. She dug her heels into the plush carpet and held her ground.

"Maybe we should reschedule," one of the men suggested.

"No! I can prove the designs are mine."

"I'm losing my patience, Miss Brooks," D.H. grumbled in a

menacing tone.

The man on the left lifted a hand. "Hold on a minute, Barry. I want to hear what she has to say."

Thank goodness!

D.H. was reluctant to let her go. Kate yanked her arm from his grasp.

"Thank you. I've spent three weeks working on these designs. Last night, I made major changes." She took a gamble that the moron had not taken the time to view her presentation before stealing it. "I can describe every slide in this presentation without viewing them."

Turning to Riesman, she challenged, "Can you?"

"Well...um," he coughed and sputtered.

The man sitting on the right picked up the remote control and motioned toward the screen. "Please, Barry. Go right ahead. We'll hear your detailed version of the next slide first." He sat back in the chair, appearing impartial.

Kate crossed her arms over her chest and waited for the fun to begin.

"I...uh. I don't remember which slide is next."

All eyes turned to her.

"That's okay. I do." She proceeded to describe the next ten slides in succession. Riesman slumped down into a chair, biding his time.

"Impressive, Miss Brooks." The client seemed to be happy with her work. Relief washed through Kate, bringing her confidence back with it.

Their attention focused on D.H. once again. "What's going on here, Barry?"

He stumbled through a lame explanation and finished up by saying it didn't matter because the designs were created by

Riesman Designs and belonged to the company until purchased by a client.

The clients no longer seemed happy. The two men wore matching scowls when they turned back to her. "Miss Brooks."

Kate laid it all on the line. She told them how D.H. had seduced her into staying by offering the world on a silver platter. Explained what she'd given up. Grabbing a piece of paper, she scribbled her cell phone number and email address, passing it over to the man on the right, who she'd learned was Travis Lundy.

"What will you do now, Kate?" Aiden McCarthy asked.

"I'll be starting my own business once my head stops spinning." She shot D.H. a demeaning glance before continuing. "What Barry has failed to realize is he didn't have an opportunity to copyright the designs you've seen today, therefore, I'll be taking them with me. I'd be thrilled to work with your organization."

The pair glanced at each other before rising. Mr. McCarthy handed her a business card. "Will there be any problems with transferring the designs?"

"Of course there will be," D.H. muttered. Mr. Lundy silenced him with one hard look.

"No." She picked up a nearby phone and called Tink into the room, giving her instructions on filing the necessary paperwork. D.H. attempted to throw a wrench in things by threatening to fire Tink.

Kate merely smiled. "That's okay. There's a better position available for her in my company."

Kate shook hands with the two men and the deal was sealed.

"Call us after you get settled. We love your work and

haven't found anyone else capable of capturing the image our organization wishes to present."

Tink hooted and gave her a high five. D.H. groaned. When word spread through the design community about him trying to pass off someone else's work as his own, he'd be watching his business going down the drain. Kate stood there, stunned. In the blink of an eye, her life had done a one-hundred-eighty degree spin.

No sooner had the clients cleared the door than Tink shot off a volley of questions.

"What's my title? How much are you going to pay me? Oh, hey. Are we moving? If so, when?" She paused only long enough to take a breath. "Have you thought of a name for the company? I've got a few ideas. Does this mean you're going after Jesse?"

"Tink," Kate pleaded, "give me a break." She considered the unfolding events. "Don't give up your job here. It will take time before I can open my own firm and afford to pay anyone. I'll figure it all out, but no, I'm not going after Jesse. I let that ship sail without me."

What a miserable mistake it had been, too. Lord, she'd screwed up her life royally. Turned her back on love and the potential of where it might lead. A wonderful man willing to give her the moon and stars. Someone she trusted. The possibility they'd get married one day.

And for what? To climb the corporate ladder. For a stressful job working for a total backstabbing dickhead. Seeking to advance a career she no longer enjoyed. Then watching it all go down the shitter.

The last words Jesse had said to her came back to haunt Kate now. *I hope the money and prestige keep you warm at night and prove to be good company.*

Money, prestige and career made poor bedfellows indeed.

The satisfaction of a job well done and pride in her work didn't even come close to how his love had made her feel. Jesse lifted her up, allowing her to walk on air.

He'd been generous beyond compare, giving her things she'd not even dreamed of. Unconditional love. Respect. Friendship. Devotion. Joy.

He'd set her free with unrestrained passion beyond her wildest dreams.

And she'd thrown it all away.

In hindsight she saw how he'd made her his top priority, putting her first. Instead of reciprocating, she'd put him second. Her career had been her primary concern when he didn't immediately give her what she wanted. A career which no longer existed until she managed to open her own firm, but there was no turning back. No do-overs. Even though Kate wanted to run straight to him, Jesse would not take her back after how badly she'd hurt and treated him.

She would rise above the ashes, making her way to the top once again with a new business of her own. Pick up the pieces and carry on.

Too bad she had not known how lonely it was at the top. Maybe then she would have cherished Jesse's generous love before it was gone.

Chapter Nineteen

"I'm on top of it. You worry about taking care of things on your end. See ya in a few hours."

Jesse caught the tail end of Brock's conversation and watched as the other man snapped is cell phone closed with a frustrated sigh. "Is there a problem?"

Damn, Jesse sure hoped there was. Driving out into the middle of nowhere to pick up a horse was not a task he looked forward to. Savannah, Brock and he would be cooped up in the truck with nothing to do but talk or think. For the past month he'd avoided both activities. His friends all wanted to discuss what had gone wrong with Kate, and his thoughts always drifted to her, but to what end. What's done is done. He had to move on.

"Nope. No problem. The seller will have the horse all set to go by the time we get there."

Crap!

"Good. I'll hitch the trailer. You wanna go see if Van is ready to leave?"

Brock grinned. "She was busy picking out CDs for the ride. I'm sure she'll be out soon."

"Oh, great," he groaned. Why the hell did Van insist he go on this trip? Brock was more than capable of handling the horse. He'd never needed help trailering an animal before.

I just need you there, Van had stated. *I feel it in my gut.* Then she'd pulled out the big ammo and used her pet name for him. *Please, Jesse James!*

Those two sentences had effectively shot down any argument he may have made. They all respected Van's instincts and visions. If she said he needed to go on this trip, then the matter was settled. He'd do anything for his friend. A few hours of his time wasn't much to ask.

Speak of the devil. Savannah stepped out onto the porch surrounded by chattering females. Millie, Steph, Sandy, Tamara and even young Mandy were all talking a mile-a-minute, trying to be heard above the others.

Jesse's stomach rolled and tension filled his body. They were up to something. A quick glance at the cat-that-ate-the-canary grin on Brock's face revealed his friend was in on whatever it was.

"Keep an eye on Cord and Riley for me. Don't let those two get into any trouble while I'm gone." Van hugged the other women goodbye.

"Jeez, Van. It's not like we're leaving for days on end. We'll be back in a few hours."

Savannah turned to face him, hands resting over the growing curve of her belly. "It's going to be one hell of a long trip if you act like a grump the whole time," she scolded.

"Hey, you're welcome to stay home. Brock and I can pick up the beast and get it back here in one piece. Then we don't have to worry about watching out for you, preggo."

"Mind your manners or I'll mind 'em for ya!"

The menacing snarl came from behind him. Jesse didn't have to turn around to know it was Van's overprotective husband.

"Let's get this over with." Jesse was already anticipating kicking back in the bunkhouse with a beer when they got back. He climbed into the back seat of the Hummer, stretched out his legs and pulled his hat down over his eyes. If he was lucky, he'd nap through the whole ride. Best laid plans...

Van poked her finger into his shoulder, over and over, while chattering worse than a magpie. The damn woman wouldn't shut up or take a hint. He didn't want to be part of the idle racket, but she offered no quarter. Whenever his end of the conversation lagged, she ground that damn finger into a tender spot of flesh.

Brock turned onto a dirt road. They drove the last five minutes in blessed silence.

"We're here," Brock stated.

Jesse yawned and glanced around as they climbed out of the truck. Something wasn't right. They were parked before a small cabin with nothing else in sight. No stables, barn, horse or seller.

"Where the hell is here?" He stretched cramped muscles. "I think you must have made a wrong turn somewhere, Brock."

"Nope. This is the right place," Van confirmed. "He's supposed to be around back. You gotta walk a short ways to find the clearing where the corral is." She handed him a lead rope. "Brock, I want you to get the trailer opened while Jesse fetches the horse."

Bossy little wench. Okay, so she owned the ranch and signed his paycheck, but damn. She didn't have to be pushy. He muttered curses under his breath, atrophied muscles protesting each movement. It did feel good to be out of the truck though.

Strolling over the property, Jesse's mind began to pick

apart the bizarre situation. Where the hell was the seller? If he were selling a horse, he'd sure be there to complete the sale and take the money. It wasn't as if there were many places out here to go either. He had not seen another building for miles around. And where on earth was this damn corral? He'd been walking forever. There was no barn or stable. No clearing. No corral. He stopped to further ponder things, tapping the rope against his thigh. A knot of dread formed in his abdomen, and Jesse figured he was about to find out whatever his friends had been up to.

To hell with this! He turned and headed back.

"There's no horse or corral back there. You've been bamboozled," he called out as he walked into the yard and froze, staring at a lot of nothing.

The truck, trailer and his friends were gone.

The sneaky bastards had left him stranded. Jesse started kicking at the ground and yelling. "Fuck! I would've been more than happy to go hide out on my hill. You didn't have to dump me off by myself. Jerks!"

"Jesse?"

The sound of the door creaking open hadn't penetrated the fog of his anger, but her voice did. He spun around to face the cabin and the woman standing on the porch. She seemed confused, yet in that moment everything became clear to him.

"We've been set up."

Kate wanted to rip Tink to shreds then hug her to pieces. A lot of fast talking had led to an impromptu vacation. Some time to regroup and get out of the "funk" she had fallen into.

If depression and self pity hadn't clouded her judgment, Kate would have seen this coming. Tink's insistence on making all the arrangements and claims of knowing the perfect place to unwind. Ugh!

When they arrived, Tink popped the trunk and told Kate to carry her bags inside while she gathered her own. No sooner had the door closed behind her than she heard the car engine roar to life. She'd made it back outside to see the taillights round a curve in the road.

Back inside, she discovered a kitchen stocked with enough supplies to last for weeks. The bedroom was dominated by a huge bed, on the corner of which sat several of the latest adult gadgets from Tink's online toy store.

Hearing Jesse's angry voice in the yard had stopped her heart from beating. When she'd opened the door and saw him, Kate had wanted to throw herself into his arms. Instead, she devoured him with her gaze. Unable to hold back any longer, she called his name.

He was such a sight for sore eyes—tall, strong and handsome as ever.

"Katie!"

The way he said her name, the one whispered word filled with hunger and need, made the blasted nickname sound divine to her ears. She stood there, paralyzed by fear and longing, afraid to hope.

"C'mere, honey."

Before her mind gave the command, her body was hurtling across the distance until Jesse's arms opened wide and pulled her in close. He held her so tightly she couldn't breathe, but it didn't matter. She'd been welcomed into his arms and it was the most wonderful haven she'd ever known.

"Oh, God," he moaned. "Need you!"

Their lips parted, mouths fused, tongues twining together.

It was a hard kiss. Demanding. Possessive. Glorious. Their bodies clung, arms binding, hands grasping. The past melted away. Hurt and pain dissolved leaving a burning desire.

They stumbled up the steps, over the porch and into the cabin, maintaining close contact, neither one willing to let go. Once inside, Jesse slammed the door and began removing her clothes.

"Jesse... Wait... We have to talk." Each word was gasped out between frantic kisses. "I'm sorry... Messed up bad... Should've..."

His mouth covered hers in a punishing kiss, stopping her from talking. When he finally pulled back, Jesse tenderly cradled her face in his hands.

"We have a lot to work out. Issues of trust, forgiveness, and accepting feelings. Problems to solve with location. That will all come later." His heavy-lidded eyes darkened. "I'm going to die if I don't get my cock buried as far into your pussy as humanly possible in the next few seconds."

"Yes, Jesse." She tore at the clothes keeping them apart. Her body was on fire, breasts swollen, nipples achy, labia drenched with hot arousal. "Hurry!"

Kate yanked her top over her head. Jesse did the same, barely allowing room to accomplish the task. She fought with the button of his jeans until he took over, opening the fastener and thrusting the material down his legs. They worked on her jeans together.

Jesse yanked her jeans down and moved to kneel, she presumed to pull them off, but got twisted in his own forgotten pants. They fell to the floor in a tangle of limbs, laughing happily, but her laughter came to an abrupt halt when his naked body came down on top of hers.

"Kate!" He stroked damp strands of hair from her face. "I

can't go slow. It's been too long."

She stared up into his face. Warm eyes, stubble darkened jaw, reddened lips. The man she loved. Kate made a silent vow not to let anything come between them again.

"Fuck slow. I want you in me. Now, Jesse!" She didn't want or need foreplay or other titillation. Kate was wet, aching and ready.

Jesse's lower body lifted and she spread her legs wide to receive him. As the satiny head of his cock probed her entrance, Kate moaned, and then cried in ecstasy as he drilled into her with one hard thrust.

They didn't pause to revel in the sensation. Both began to move their hips in a counter rhythm, slamming into the other. His hands were everywhere—plumping her breasts, tweaking nipples, tormenting her clit. She reclaimed his body in turn— nails scoring his back, kneading his ass, touching everywhere she could reach.

Sweat slicked flesh smacked together noisily. Each withdrawal brought its own slurping sounds as her muscles fought to keep him deep within her body. It was raw, primal and completely amazing.

"Jesse. Yessss!" She hung on the precipice, bracing herself for the explosive orgasm she felt building.

"Kate," he moaned. "Come for me."

The words were a firm order. A dominant command which should rankle, but had the opposite effect. She loved when he took control of their lovemaking, liberating her to simply feel. His arms wrapped around her legs, lifting her ass off the floor. In this new position, his pelvis ground against her clit with each powerful thrust. Once, twice...

Extreme pleasure burst through her clit, spreading out through her body. Every muscle spasmed. It was too much. A scream rumbled in her chest, but caught in her throat, escaping as a gurgling sound.

Hot blasts of come pummeled her womb as Jesse's climax hit. He hollered her name, gave a few weak pumps then collapsed on top of her. His welcomed weight crushed her into the floor and Kate couldn't have been happier until he placed butterfly kisses all over her sweaty face and whispered words of love. His expression was serious as he stared down into her eyes, making her tremble.

"Marry me, Kate. I don't care where we live. I love you and want us to be together."

Her heart stuttered, then raced erratically. She'd wanted those three words, the commitment of marriage, for so long. Had left him behind when they hadn't been offered.

She felt content knowing they would face the challenge of accepting each other for who they are and working toward a shared life with open arms and hearts. The future suddenly looked bright.

"Answer me."

The demand thrilled her. There was the burst of dominant lover she'd missed. Her heart beat so fast she was afraid it might rupture. Kate wound her fingers into his damp hair and pulled Jesse down for a kiss. "Yes," she breathed against his lips. "Yes to marriage and the ranch. Yes to kids, but not for a while yet. Yes to us—whatever it takes and wherever the road leads."

"I love you so much!"

The wealth of emotions passing between them touched her soul in miraculous ways. She would put him first, never taking his love for granted again. It had been a hard lesson.

"I love you, Jesse. You are my world. My everything. I plan

on spending the rest of my life showing you how much you mean to me."

Epilogue

"Unfuckingbelieveable!"

Brock Madden slammed his fist down on the dashboard. He'd been outwitted by two conniving women. Tamara and Van were going to pay when he caught up with them. This whole thing was supposed to be about Jesse. The poor schmuck had wandered around the ranch in a depressed haze for too long. An intervention had been Tamara's idea. Riley, the damn prankster, had filled in the how.

All their friends had come together to "help" Jesse. They'd drawn Brock into this and played him all along, stranding him with the one woman who had the power to drive him to drink.

Prunella Lucretia St. Claire-Fitzmoore, better know as Tink. Privately referred to by many names, including psycho bitch.

"Turn right," he instructed when they reached the highway.

"Uh-unh. I'm heading east."

The obstinate witch made him want to pull out all his hair and scream. He glanced at her long blonde locks streaked with shades of red, from pink to burgundy and got a better idea. He'd pull on her hair while thrusting his cock into that foul, gorgeous mouth. Hey, it would shut her up. With her lips stretched over his shaft she wouldn't be half as annoying.

"Look, Pruney..."

WHAP!

She let go of the steering wheel and slapped his cheek so hard Brock's ears rang. "Don't ever call me that."

"Okay, Tink," he ground from between clenched teeth. "It's getting late and Denver is a full day's drive. At least eight hours. The ranch is only about two hours away. If we go to the ranch, you can get rid of me quicker."

"True." The car idled at the stop sign as she considered the dilemma. "Or I could dump your ass at the first gas station we find, thus expediting your departure from my car, Tex."

There she went with the Tex bullshit again. "I'm not from Texas!"

"Whatever." Her hand waved in the air dismissively. "If you prefer Dick, it's fine with me."

His blood boiled in his veins and Brock saw red. Anger was good. He was prepared to deal with intense desire to choke the shit out of the psycho wench. What he had a difficult time with was the alarming, all-consuming compulsion to fuck her into next week.

It was beyond reason—difficult to control. His cock lengthened, eager to abandon the confines of his pants and invade the hot clasp of her pussy.

He tugged at his hat and rubbed his jaw with a clenched fist. There was some inherent flaw in his DNA. Had to be. What other possibility was there? Unless...

Maybe it was a mental defect. There wasn't any history of mental illness in his family, but that meant squat if he was deranged. Chances were he was bi-polar or had the dual personality thing like that Sybil chick. It justified the dichotomy of both hating and desiring her.

Yup, a majorly warped mental psychosis sounded

reasonable. Pretty scary stuff to be relieved by the realization one was insane as an explanation for being attracted to someone. Only attraction was too simple of a word. What he felt for the psycho bitch was closer to obsessive lust.

"How 'bout we drop the name calling and get the hell out of here before Jesse or Kate come after us."

Tink drummed her fingers on the steering wheel. Lameass Tex did odd things to her. In the shock of finding out he'd been stranded at the remote cabin, she hadn't protested when he climbed into her car. After all, she didn't want to mess up the intervention they'd painstakingly arranged for Jesse and Kate.

Tamara must have had something to do with this bull. The more Tink thought about it, the more convinced she became. They'd only spoken on the phone, but it had been clear the woman was devious. How the other woman had known there was something between Tex and her was anyone's best guess. Maybe Kate had inadvertently given the others some clue.

The way Tink saw it, she had two options. Drive like the wind and get rid of the big pain-in-the-ass was one choice. The other was to rip his clothes off and ride the cowboy until the fire burning between her legs subsided. Her mind screamed for the former while her body ached for the latter.

Her nipples were hard, pebbled points. With each breath her lacy bra abraded them, sending tingling jolts into her abdomen. Her denuded pussy lips were swollen and slick. In fact, if she got any wetter there was going to be a huge stain on the car seat.

Left or right? The indecision was making her antsy.

If she headed towards home, she still had the option of losing him somewhere or taking him captive. Visions of tying him to her bed and riding him to satiation flashed in her head. The man was built from stone. All hard, rippling muscle under tanned skin. Mapping each bulge and dip over his chiseled flesh with her tongue would provide days of delicious distraction.

And he had the cutest mustache. Maybe she'd take a ride on it. She had never been with a man who had a mustache before.

If she headed towards the ranch, the same two options existed. Leave him there and haul ass or maybe let him tie her to his bed. She'd bet high stakes Brock knew delightful ways to play with rope.

The ranch was sounding better. Hell, Kate had endlessly prattled on about all the delicious eye candy on the Shooting Star Ranch. There were several virile, strapping cowboys there capable of slaking her lusts. Maybe a bit of group action could be arranged.

Decision made, she shifted into first gear and spun the wheel clockwise. Time to cowboy up!

About the Author

To learn more about Nicole Austin, please visit www.nicoleaustin.net. Send an email to Nicole at nicoleaustinsizzles@yahoo.com or sign up for her Yahoo! group to join in the fun with other readers as well as Nicole! http://groups.yahoo.com/group/ TandA_FantasyPlayground/

*Workin' up a hot, sticky sweat is pure pleasure with a
hard-ridin' cowboy...or two.*

Rode Hard, Put Up Wet
© 2007 Lorelei James

Struggling stock contractor Gemma Jansen swallows her pride and tracks down circuit rider Cash Big Crow to offer him a job managing her ranch. Cash agrees on one condition: theirs won't be strictly a working relationship. She's the boss during the day, but once she's corralled in the bedroom, Cash calls the shots. Despite concerns about their age difference, Gemma consents.

Cash suspects the sexy widow hides an untapped wild streak. He intends to loosen her tightly held reins of control—even if he has to break out his horsewhip to do it.

But Cash is in for a surprise. Gemma proves a rough and ready participant in any leather-n-lace game Cash dreams up.

Between riding herd on his wayward daughter, Macie, and rowdy cowboy Carter McKay doggin' Macie's every boot step, Cash struggles to hide his true feelings for Gemma—except this time, Gemma's grabbed the bull by the horns and she's playing for keeps.

Summer's going to be a hot one at the Bar 9.

Warning: this book contains: explicit sex nine ways 'til Sunday—including ménage a trois, inventive use of ropes, naughty girls getting spanked, stubborn men getting hog-tied, graphic language and whoo-wee! hot nekkid cowboy on cowboy action.

Available now in ebook and print from Samhain Publishing.

GET IT NOW

MyBookStoreAndMore.com

GREAT EBOOKS, GREAT DEALS . . . AND MORE!

Don't wait to run to the bookstore down the street, or
waste time shopping online at one of the "big boys." Now,
all your favorite Samhain authors are all in one place—at
MyBookStoreAndMore.com. Stop by today and discover
great deals on Samhain—and a whole lot more!

Samhain publishing, ltd

WWW.SAMHAINPUBLISHING.COM

GREAT
cheap
fun

Discover eBooks!

THE FASTEST WAY TO GET THE HOTTEST NAMES

Get your favorite authors on your favorite reader, long before they're out in print! Ebooks from Samhain go wherever you go, and work with whatever you carry—Palm, PDF, Mobi, and more.

samhain
publishing, ltd

WWW.SAMHAINPUBLISHING.COM

Printed in the United Kingdom
by Lightning Source UK Ltd.
133225UK00001B/105/P